RIO

RIO

by

Clayton Nash

Dales Large Print Books
Long Preston, North Yorkshire,
BD23 4ND, England.

British Library Cataloguing in Publication Data.

Nash, Clayton
    Rio.

A catalogue record of this book is
available from the British Library

ISBN   1-84262-391-5 pbk C| 52616179

First published in Great Britain 2004 by Robert Hale Limited

Copyright © Clayton Nash 2004

Cover illustration © Longaron by arrangement with
Norma Editorial S.A.

The right of Clayton Nash to be identified as the author of this
work has been asserted by him in accordance with the
Copyright, Designs and Patents Act, 1988

Published in Large Print 2005 by arrangement with
Robert Hale Limited

Dales Large Print is an imprint of Library Magna Books Ltd.

Printed and bound in Great Britain by
T.J. (International) Ltd., Cornwall, PL28 8RW

CHAPTER 1

GRINGO

The sweating horse came up over the steep part of the high trail, blowing and snorting, beginning to show signs of rebellion. The rider savvied how the big sorrel must feel: it had been pushed and pushed hard these past hours – and he had pushed himself just as hard. For longer, too.

The hot Sonora sun blasted him from pale sandstone boulders and he squinted hard grey eyes in a face that was sun-blackened, the crows' feet around those eyes radiating out in paler streaks as he swept the land before him. He held the rifle across his thighs, ready to bring it into instant use if he spotted Barnaby.

The son of a bitch must be suffering more

than he was right now and that was fine with the rider. Man hires your talents and your gear, you expect him to pay without demur when the time comes. Instead – well, here he was on a damn manhunt, trying to run down the cheat who had arrived in Los Sequito so arrogantly three days earlier and presented himself at the door of the freight office.

'Howdy – they told me a gringo was running a freight line here. And he's also a hunting guide. That makes you the one they call "Rio", right?'

'They call me that,' the freighter admitted, frowning a little as he looked up from his lading bills. Even sitting down he looked tall. Tall and rangy, whip-lean, rawhide muscles bulging his shirt at the shoulders, showing on his forearms where he had the sleeves rolled up to the elbows. A working man, not just a pen-pusher. The face was square, clean-shaven, unsmiling, the grey eyes searching – and not particularly liking what they saw.

The newcomer introduced himself as 'Barnaby' – 'You can call me *Mister* Barnaby. I don't use first names with people I hire.'

'Maybe we'll get around to just what I'll call you later, but what can I do for you right now?'

'Goddamn train broke down at Chinapa. Some indispensable copper pipe that can't be obtained for a couple of days – 'bout what you'd expect in this lousy *mañana* land.'

The man called Rio waited impatiently.

'Yeah – well, I couldn't see myself twiddling my thumbs for a couple of days in a dump like Chinapa, so I asked around and the most interesting thing I learned was about you being a part-time hunting guide.'

Barnaby, a hefty man, solid not fat, smiled crookedly, as if waiting for some sign of approval from Rio. He got nothing but a blank stare. And silence.

'Look, *amigo,* I'm a hunter – among other things. Perhaps I'd better tell you I run a big cattle spread up there in Texas, the B Bar B. Likely you've heard of it.'

Rio nodded slightly.

'Maybe you even widelooped a few of my cows,' Barnaby said slyly, a mild nastiness in his tone. 'I hear you aren't averse to such – adventures.'

'Don't believe all you hear. Then keep it to yourself. You ever gonna get to the point?'

Barnaby sighed. 'Guess freighting must pay pretty well, huh? Otherwise you'd be more civil to a potential customer.'

'Customers get good service from me. That's what they pay for. They take my personality along with it or they go elsewhere.'

Barnaby coloured. 'Jesus, you must be doing mighty good!' He looked around at the drab office and beyond through a smeared glass panel into a big warehouse that showed dust-moted sun's rays slanting through loose roof shingles and gaps in the walls, where clapboards had been mated none too well with the adobe. He glimpsed a couple of wagons, some Mexicans loading one and taking their time about it. 'Not that you *show* how well you're doing, but I savvy that.' He winked. 'Don't pay to let everyone know you're pocketin' the *dinero*. Smart move, especially down here with these greasers.'

'Look, Barnaby–'

'*Mister* Barnaby!'

'Barnaby,' Rio said flatly, his eyes steady and unflinching. 'I'm busy – you want to tell me your life story I mightn't be averse to meeting you in the *cantina* for a yarn over a drink or two, but right now I don't have the time. So…'

Rio glanced towards the street door.

Barnaby's eyes narrowed and his jaw muscles knotted. 'I want to hunt a grizzly – they tell me they come big and black down here and I'd like one for my den wall.'

'Chihuahua's the only state in Mexico with grizzly bear. You can find black bear and whitetail deer, the odd mountain lion or peccaries here in Sonora, but not grizzlies.'

'OK – so we go to Chihuahua. It's not that far from here. I'll pay double your usual fee.'

Rio looked at him sharply. 'You must want

that grizzly mighty bad.'

'I want it – and I usually get what I want. Like I said, I'm prepared to pay.' He curled a lip. 'I'm used to being stuck with high prices, but I demand high quality.'

Rio set down the bills-of-lading and the pencil. Barnaby smiled crookedly.

'Got your attention, huh?'

'You have, but depends when you want to go. And it won't be any quick ride across, *bang!* and the grizzly's ready for skinning-out and stuffing. They're hard to find.'

'That's what I'm paying you for. Find me one. A big one. Record size.'

Rio pursed thin lips. 'Tall order. But if you've got a week…'

'Christ, man, I've got a cattle ranch to run! I can give you three days, four if I stretch it, no more. If you're as good as I hear, you ought to be able to do it.'

Rio stared a while and then nodded gently. 'Might manage it in three days. But it'll cost you – they try to protect the grizzly population down here, which may come as a surprise, but it's true. I guess you don't have your own guns with you?'

Barnaby shook his head. 'No, damn the luck – wasn't expecting to do any hunting. Got custom–made Mannlicher bolt-actions at home that'll take the head clear off any animal walking this continent. What can you offer?'

'Well, the Mexican authorities are a little leery of high-powered weapons – too tempting for someone to try a long-range assassination of some governor or even *El Presidente*. Mostly we're limited to saddle guns – but a twelve-gauge Greener loaded with Brenneke ball would stop most grizzlies.'

Barnaby looked startled. 'A shotgun? Man, I don't aim to get *that* goddamn close to any grizzly!'

'I've got a couple of Mauser bolt actions. I've done a little work on them and they'll take a .44 with an extra big charge, and if you use a dum-dum bullet it'll probably knock down a grizz.'

'*Probably!* Hell, man, you like to lose

clients? I want more of a guarantee than that!'

Rio shrugged. 'Up to you. I'm risking my neck, too. I can't get you a licence to kill a grizzly in Chihuahua. We'll have to do this kind of sneaky.'

Barnaby snorted. 'So, you're already upping the price, huh? Well, I'm no piker if I get what I go after, so you better be up to it, Rio!'

'I'll do what I can for you,' the gringo said slowly. 'It'll be my best – if it's not good enough...'

He let it hang.

Barnaby's face closed. 'It better had be good enough or you an' me're gonna have something of a diff-i-culty!'

The threat didn't' seem to worry Rio.

Now here he was hunting the man, not the grizzly that Barnaby had wounded and then run off and left to suffer and rampage across Chihuahua in a murderous rage, while the pain and infection ate into its huge body,

14

turning it into an almost unstoppable killing machine.

He should have realized that Barnaby was one of those hunters who did all his shooting from long range. No ethical tracking and stalking and facing the animal on its own ground, or using skill and courage to make the kill. No, he even asked – *expected* – Rio to flush the bear for him, then drive it though a narrow cleft in the rocks where Barnaby would be waiting amidst the safety of some boulders, above the trail the bear could be expected to take, ball-loaded shotgun at the ready. But he chose to use the inadequate, modified Mauser, despite Rio's warning it wouldn't do the job on a bear this size. Later he said he hadn't wanted to damage the hide with a large-calibre Brenneke ball, and had tried for a brain shot, merely wounding the bear and putting out one of its eyes. Which, of course, drove it berserk.

He used the shotgun after that, but by then he was in a panic and both barrels missed the fatal spots. One ripped open the bear's side just below his hip, likely tearing up part of his stomach. Rio had never heard such an unearthly blood-chilling scream come from any animal as that grizzly had loosed across the Chihuahua mountains.

By then Rio was dragging the terrified Barnaby away from the boulders that the blood-spattered bear was tearing out of the landscape in its agony.

They had both been lucky to get away with whole hides, though one of the pack horses had had its neck snapped by the bear and its guts strewn across the slope. Both the shotgun and the rifle had been lost as well as a carton of Rio's hand-loaded ammunition.

'Yeah, well, don't expect me to pay for them!' Barnaby snapped a long time later when Rio judged they were finally safe from the rampaging bear – although, way in the distance, they could still hear an occasional agonized scream.

That was when the trouble started. Barnaby figured because he didn't get his trophy, any loss of equipment had to be borne by Rio.

'Don't work that way, Barnaby,' Rio told him: he never had used the *Mister* term Barnaby had demanded. 'You lose the guns and ammo, you pay for them. The packhorse – well, he was a good'n, but it was his own fault when he panicked and ran plumb into the bear's path. I'll carry that.'

'Damn big of you! But you'll carry the loss of the guns, too. I'm not paying for them.'

Rio set down the Winchester he had just loaded and stood, facing Barnaby on the banks of the narrow stream where they had camped.

'Looks like that diff-i-culty you mentioned has arrived.'

Barnaby snorted, held out a hand, fingers spread. 'Don't make the mistake of taking me on in a brawl, Rio! Don't make that mistake! I've travelled all over the world and I've been instructed in the Queensbury Rules and method of prize-fighting. You'll rue the damn day you tangle with me if you're stupid enough to try it.'

'Seems to be the only way I'm gonna make you see your obligations,' Rio said and punched Barnaby squarely in the middle of the face.

That's what he aimed to do, leastways. But Barnaby's head wasn't where it was supposed to be and his fist slid across the tip of the man's left shoulder. Rio just had time to notice this when three fast, successive blows almost took his head off. He staggered, felt a leg go out to one side and instinctively put down a hand on the slope.

Barnaby bared his white teeth and brought up a roundhouse swing that took Rio on the right ear, making the bells ring and the birds sing a frantic, discordant song. He went all the way down and rolled away from the expected boots. But Barnaby was dancing around him, fists and forearms in front of face and upper body. He laughed briefly as Rio thrust up, raging, and went in swinging. There was a short weaving dance and then

Barnaby was almost standing on Rio's toes as he slugged him in the body and head and twisted his own big body to lend force to a blow that seemed to make Rio's ribs cave in. He sucked in air sharply, stumbled, and went down again, his jaw feeling as if it had been kicked by a mule with a bellyful of green berries. Rio shook his head, ears ringing more wildly than ever, vision doubled, the taste of blood in his throat.

Once again Barnaby was standing in that strange pose with arched back and fists and forearms raised, dancing about, waiting for Rio to either get up or slump back to the ground. From this level, Rio could see that Barnaby's ribs were unprotected from the side and back.

He was hurting but he knew he would hurt a lot more if Barnaby kept getting the upper hand. So he rolled suddenly a little way down slope, stopped, swung his legs around and bounded to his feet, releasing an involuntary grunt with effort as he lunged back at Barnaby.

The man was not expecting an attack from that quarter, started to turn but slipped on the slope and that was all Rio needed. Two bone-shattering blows slammed into Barnaby's ribs on the right side, from the back, and breath gusted out of him, his whole body shuddering with the impact. Before he could recover, Rio was behind him, driving a tattoo of punches up and down his spine, the back of his neck, the kidney region. Barnaby was hurled forward, too fast and too violently to stay on his feet. He went down to his knees, skidding, his fine trousers tearing on the gravel.

Rio was beside him in a flash, arms working like pistons and, in less than two minutes – a long time for any man to take a battering from unrelenting fists – Barnaby was stretched out on his back, face bloody and bruised and swelling in several places, one eye closing, lips split, at least one white tooth broken off at the gum line. Bloody mucus smeared across from his nostrils and blood dripped from his chin which looked to be lopsided.

He managed to get a hand in front of his shattered face, gurgling unintelligible words until he spat some blood. Then Rio heard him say, *''Nough!* 'Nough – damn – you!'

Rio, gasping and breathing hard, pointed to Barnaby's torn shirt. 'I can see your money belt – get it off and start counting.'

Barnaby was slow obeying, but Rio gave him the time. He knew the man was beaten. What was more, Barnaby knew it, too.

But while Rio was checking the greenbacks, Barnaby spun away and slid down the slope to where Rio's six gun had fallen unnoticed from his holster.

Rio dived away as the man's hands closed on the gun and he rolled on to his back and triggered. The shot blasted through the mountains and Rio staggered as lead burned across his right hip. His leg collapsed under him and he fell sprawling, within arm's reach of his rifle. Barnaby saw the man lunging for it and his eyes widened as he fired again, wildly, leapt up and ran to where the horses waited under the trees.

He slammed into leather and as he fought the horse around, snapped another shot down at Rio who was sprawled full-length on the ground now, working the lever of the rifle. Barnaby was spurring away when Rio fired and he saw the man lurch wildly, almost falling out of the saddle.

The six-gun fell and he straightened, raking with the spurs, driving the horse on into encroaching night. Rio sent another shot after him, knowing he would miss, then picked up the six gun and staggered back to the camp. He knelt by the stream and pulled out his shirt, dropped his trousers and examined the wound across his hip and buttock. A long, curving line, shallow, luckily, but bleeding plenty.

He would patch it up as best he could and then he would have to start looking for Barnaby. He couldn't leave even a sorry son of a bitch like him to wander these mountains wounded – and with a murderous grizzly still on the prowl.

It came with the job.

You guided a hunter into the wilderness and you brought him out again – preferably alive.

But you didn't lose him. Not for any reason. Not ever.

And not if you valued your reputation.

Especially if you were a gringo living in Mexico because you daren't go back to the United States and about all you really had left was your good reputation.

'God damn you, Barnaby! he murmured as he began what he knew was going to be a long, dangerous search. 'God – damn – you!'

CHAPTER 2

JUGADOR

Rio was just seeing off a wagon of freight, south to Madera, his gringo sidekick, Zutano, in the driving seat. The name meant So-and-So and Zutano claimed he had earned it from his father who always called him a 'Lousy little so-and-so'. When he was twelve, tired of his father's trouser belt laying criss-cross patterns over his back and legs, he ran him through with a pitchfork and headed south of the Border and had lived in Mexico ever since. To this day he didn't know if his brutal father had survived the pitchfork or not – and what's more, he professed he didn't damn well care.

He was a good wagoneer, could handle the roughest of the half-wild mules and horses

24

they used in the teams. And he could fight when he had to – sometimes when he *felt* like it – could charm women of all ages from four to sixty, and had done so on several occasions, and had a weakness for tequila. But when he was working he stayed mostly sober and got his freight in on time.

Rio lit a cigarillo as he watched the wagon and its two Mexican outriders disappear over the rise and turned back into the adobe building where his office was situated.

Two men were waiting for him. Two *hombres imporantes*. One was the *alcalde*, the mayor of Los Sequito, and the other was a mean-eyed *mestizo* who went by the name of Jugador, which meant 'gambler', and as he ran all games of chance in the town – and beyond – it was appropriate.

The mayor was a small man, neatly dressed, smelling slightly of some kind of perfume. It could be some he had used himself or the remnants from one of his many mistresses who had visited him recently. He sported a small, pencil-line moustache and his hands were large for such a small man. There was a little humour showing in his bright, dark eyes.

Jugador was tall and lean, wore a *pistolero* moustache and drab, dark grey suit. But his vest was flowered and intertwined with gold-thread brocade and he had a long cigarillo clamped between white teeth as he nodded to Rio when the gringo entered. *He was the one who ran things: the mayor was just a front, though they hid it well enough.*

Rio wasn't pleased to see either of them or that they had helped themselves to his liquor. He got himself a glass and poured some of his Kentucky bourbon and drank half before turning to the waiting men.

'*Buenos días, amigos* – now what the hell do you want? I've got a lot of work to do.'

'*Sí,* we realize you are a busy man, Rio,' said the little mayor. 'But you were able to take time off recently for a hunting trip to Chihuahua, no?'

Rio swore gently under his breath, hoping they hadn't seen the slight pause as he raised his glass just as the mayor spoke. *How in hell did that little son of a bitch find out so many things!* There wasn't anything that happened in Sonora or Chihuahua that he didn't know about. But Rio had thought his illegal hunting trip with Barnaby had been covered well enough.

'Just a short break – to accommodate a friend, *alcalde.*'

'*Sí*, it is always good to show a friend a kindness,' acknowledged the mayor. 'But–' He paused, looked around the cluttered, dusty office and spread his short arms with the large hands at the end. 'Where is this friend? He did not ride back with you...?'

Damn the nosy little bastard! 'No – he had business back in Texas, decided to pick up a train at Ciuadad Guerrero and head straight for home.'

'Ah, *sí*. And your hunting trip – it was successful?'

They damn well knew he had been after a grizzly!

'Well, yes and no. My friend shot a grizzly,

27

which was menacing him, I might add, so that he had no other choice...'

The mayor pursed his lips and nodded understandingly. 'Of course – a legitimate kill on a protected animal without a licence. But, a man must defend himself, no?'

He glanced at the gambler but Jugador made no acknowledgement, just continued to glare at Rio with that implacable stare.

'He only wounded the grizz and we had a time of it when it ran into our camp.' Rio knew they must have noticed his slight limp and he now touched the hip wound. 'He came too damn close to me – rakes me across the butt, killed a packhorse.'

'Aieee! Too close for comfort, *amigo!* You managed to put the poor animal out of its suffering?'

Poor animal! You goddamn hypocrite! I've seen you blast squirrels and rodents until the hillside was splashed red with their corpses just to fill in time while your meal was prepared! Poor animal! Hogwash...

But, yeah – he had managed to kill the

bear. And it had almost managed to kill *him!*

Barnaby's trail wasn't hard to follow: the man had ridden out in a panic and hadn't attempted to cover his tracks. It had been just on nightfall before Rio had sighted him, riding a staggering, foam-slick horse through a series of draws edged with brush and small timber. Grizzly country!

Sure enough, that wounded bear had been there, lying in wait or simply tired from venting its rage and losing so much blood. It had charged out of the timber and slammed into Barnaby's horse, knocking man and animal to the ground. Rio was still three hundred yards away but he had heard Barnaby's scream clearly, even above the terrified shrilling of the downed horse. The bear had disemboweled the animal first, luckily for Barnaby, who had scrambled away up slope, heading into thick brush. The bear simply tore up the brush and saplings as it raged after him and Rio had ridden within rifle range then and, against his better judgement, knowing he should be closer, had put a bullet into the big hairy body. To his surprise the bear had gone down, rolling and crashing back down the slope to sprawl in a splayed heap at the bottom. Barnaby, exhausted, breathing hard, stood wide-eyed and watched as Rio rode in, levering another shell into the rifle as he approached the bear.

'It's dead by now!' croaked Barnaby. 'Surely to hell!'

Without taking his eyes off the animal, Rio slowly raised the rifle and said, 'Always shoot a dead bear – just to make sure!'

And even as the rifle crashed the bear erupted in one final burst of violence and blood lust, lunging at Rio. A swipe from a huge paw knocked him on his back and the bear swayed in, checked in mid-stride, an almost comical look on its face as its muscles finally refused to cooperate. It staggered and fell towards Rio, reaching with those ex- tended sabre-claws, determined to kill its tormentor before it died. Rio rolled to one side, thrust out the rifle – later finding the muzzle had gone into the bear's right ear –

and pulled the trigger.

This time the dead bear stayed dead.

'How'm I gonna get around now?' Barnaby said as he looked down at his gutted mount. *No 'thanks for saving my neck'; or anything even close...*

'You can ride double with me. Far as the railroad track. Flag down the next train. Ought to be one along in a couple days.'

Barnaby blanched. 'I can't wait out in the middle of nowhere in *bandido* country!'

'Anywhere is *bandido* country down here. Climb aboard and we'll get going. Big moon tonight. You could be lucky and pick up a train by tomorrow.'

Rio didn't know when – or if – Barnaby had managed to flag down a train. And he didn't damn well care, either. The man had cost him plenty. It wasn't until he was riding back to Sonora that he realized in his hurry to get after Barnaby he must have dropped the greenbacks he had forced the man to pay him. Well, too late now...

'Yeah, we managed to kill the grizzly before

he did too much damage,' he answered the mayor finally. 'No real harm done, *amigo.*'

Again the little man pursed his lips. 'I must be careful, as you know, my friend. I have – arrangements – with people in Chihuahua. If someone, like you even, *amigo,* from my town slips across and hunts illegally, it comes back on me, I must pay compensation.' Then he smiled. 'And, of course, recover it from you.'

So, it was yet another shakedown!

Rio sighed. 'I'm a mite strapped for cash right now, Mayor.'

'That why you have not paid any more instalments on your debt to *me,* Rio?' They were the first words Jugador had spoken and he said them flatly, having obviously been waiting for a chance to drop them into this conversation.

Rio looked at him steadily. 'Far as I know, I'm all paid up, Jugador.'

The gambler shook his head. 'The interest, *sí* – but there is the matter of the principal.'

Rio stiffened. 'Wait a minute! You mean what I've been paying you the past six months is only *interest?*'

Jugador shrugged. 'I must make a living, Rio. You are responsible for your men and their debts, no? Well, Zutano and Monje make the debt with me or my card dealers – you need them for an urgent trip, so I agree they can go, providing you pay the debt off.'

'Christ, I know how I got into this!' snapped Rio, frowning. 'What I didn't know was just how much of a dirty snake you could be, Jugador.'

The mayor's eyes flew wide and he jumped back a full yard, cannoning into the wall, alarmed, opening his mouth – but there was no time for words. The gambler had reacted instantly to the insult, a hand streaking to the back of his neck. Something flashed metallically as it flew across the office towards Rio.

The freighter dropped flat and heard the *cuchillo* thud into the wall, quivering. Even as he rolled across the floor another knife almost pinned his arm to the boards. He yanked hard and the cloth of the shirt sleeve ripped around the blade. Rio came up snatching a chair and the third knife Jugador kept in the special triple sheath strapped high between his shoulders quivered in the chair base – a moment before the legs smashed across the side of Jugador's head.

The gambler staggered into the wall, started to crumple, and Rio hit him again with the chair, one leg splintering this time. Jugador made a half-sigh, half-grunt and stretched out beside the desk.

Rio spun towards the mayor who was pasty-faced now, hands shoulder-high, shaking his head.

'Is not my *argumento, señor!*'

'Keep it that way, Mayor,' Rio said, tossing the broken chair aside. He looked down at the unconscious gambler. 'He's lucky I'm not wearing my gun.'

But as he spoke, he stepped over the prone body, opened his desk drawer and took out his six-gun and bullet-belt rig. He buckled it about his waist quickly.

'But I'll wear it from now on.'

The *alcade* glanced at Jugador as if to make sure the man was breathing. He was bleeding from a wound somewhere above his hairline and another on his face. Then the mayor turned his gaze on to Rio.

'A man can be too *duro* sometimes, Rio. Far too tough for his own good – I tell you this as a friend. Jugador is not a man who forgives or forgets easily.'

'That makes two of us. All right, Mayor. Why did you two come here? I've been reminded that I owe you both money – that I don't have right now. I figure you've got some way in mind for me to square my debts – like on the other occasions…?'

The mayor smiled widely and leaned forward a little. 'Exactly like on other occasions, Rio! I am pleased that you have been smart enough to recognize the fact.'

Rio swore under his breath. He might have known.

They wanted him to run another batch of wetbacks across the Rio Grande into Texas.

CHAPTER 3

TEXAS DEAL

Barnaby was back and his ramrod, a sober man named Kelly Treece, wished to hell the man had stayed down in Mexico.

Barnaby returned in about the worst frame of mind Treece had ever seen. Sour and stiff and sporting a gunshot wound he wouldn't talk about for three days. Then he told Kelly Treece the story, about hiring Rio to find him a grizzly down in Chihuahua and things going all to hell.

'Son of a bitch near got me killed!' he raged, face darkening at the memory. 'Not only put me right in the path of the goddamn bear that forced me to fire before I was ready and wound the animal, but after I finally put the thing out of its misery, this

36

Rio pulled a gun on me.'

'The hell'd he do that for?' demanded Treece, who knew from past experience how Barnaby could always embellish a story so that, whatever the truth, Barnaby came out OK.

Barnaby scowled. 'Man's loco. I think I winged him, but he got me, too, and I had to run – on foot, mind. Damn grizzly had gutted my horse ...anyway he caught me, took me near a railroad and dumped me! Had to wait nigh on two days for a goddamn rattle-trap of a Mex train and then it only took me as far as Mata Ortiz, end of the line. Had to ride a lice-riddled burro to Nuevo Casa Grandes before I picked up a proper train back to the Border...'

'You sure had it rough, boss,' commiserated Kelly Treece, caught the look in Barnaby's eye and hastily amended the 'boss' to *Mister* Barnaby.

'I did – and I don't aim to just sit still for it. You go find Luis Banda and tell him I've got a job for him.'

'Banda? Hell, that killer…?' Treece's voice started to fade as soon as he caught the look on Barnaby's face. He nodded gently. 'You're sendin' him after this Rio?'

The rancher surprised Treece by hesitating. 'Yeah. Want him to go to Bravo first, then Los Sequito. There's somethin' about this Rio – he was leery about taking me into Chihuahua and other things. I think he's hiding out down there and I want to know why…' His mouth tightened. 'If he figures he can get away with treating me like dirt he's sure in for one helluva surprise? Now go get Banda.'

There were six men to take north to the Border.

The mayor kept out of it at this stage but Jugador was right there to make arrangements. He was still mighty riled at Rio for hammering him with that chair and his face showed the marks of the conflict. But he was a businessman first and the gambler wouldn't let personal feelings get in the way of making a few easy dollars.

And running wetbacks to some of the Border ranches was lucrative and without too much risk. At least, without risk to Jugador and the mayor.

Rio was the one who had to take the chances on the journey north through country that crawled with *bandidos* and then had to face the biggest danger of all – getting them across the river safely into Texas without the Border Patrols being alerted.

And Rio made very little out of it, certainly no cash-in-hand. But this was part of the price he had to pay for holing up in Los Sequito under a fake name. He was in the hands of the *alcalde* and Jugador. It had been sheer bad luck – with a little *good* luck mixed in, he had to admit that – that both of them had found him at the edge of the desert, fever-ridden and delirious. He probably would have died but for them – and they were never going to let him forget it.

Raving, he had apparently said enough for

them to pick up on his story, even if they didn't have all the names involved. Being devious types, they had soon realized there could be considerable advantage in giving shelter to a gringo in their town, especially one handy with a gun – and who would be under their control. *That was the part he hated!*

But it worked out pretty good. Rio had to admit he had done all right since he had come to Los Sequito. He had built up his freight line into a fairly profitable business, despite Jugador and the mayor finding ways to bleed off his profits at every opportunity. He had more downs than ups but at least he was still alive and when he squared away what he owed both men there would be some kind of a reckoning before he moved on, hopefully to bigger and better things.

But right now he had to make arrangements for getting these six men north to the Rio. Because Zutano and Monje – 'Monk' – were on the trail south, it meant he was going to have to make the northern run himself. And he never felt easy about getting within spitting distance of the Border.

Holt would have paid watchers within miles of it, north and south, even after all this time. But there was no way out – he couldn't trust any of his other men on a deal like this. Anyway, most were family men and he refused to put them at risk.

'Which ranch this time?' Rio asked Jugador as the six wetbacks sat in a corner of the freight shed, bunched up, all watching this gringo they were entrusting their lives to.

Jugador glanced at the papers he held. 'B Bar B. You will be met at San Antonio de Bravo … something wrong?'

There was a hint of hope in the gambler's question as he watched Rio's face.

Barnaby! The big-time Texan, wounder of grizzlies, was nothing more than a cheapskate cowman, using wetback labour to boost his profits. The big man, Mister Barnaby. Nothing more than a penny-pinching rancher no matter how big his spread was.

Rio just hoped the man didn't realize who

would be bringing him his wetback slave-labour this time. He figured a man like Barnaby would not forget the treatment he had received down here for quite some time.

But in answer to Jugador's question, he merely said, 'Well, it means I've got to cross the Cordillera and then most of Chihuahua...'

'As usual, *amigo*.'

Rio took a closer look at the huddled Mexicans without appearing to do so. 'Must be hard-up for labour, this Barnaby.'

The gambler stiffened. 'I did not mention any names.'

'Well, most everyone knows feller named Barnaby runs the B Bar B in the Big Bend country of Texas.' It sounded a little lame, but at the same time, it was a good enough answer.

'Hmmmmm – well, you just deliver the men on time, Rio.'

'Gonna be hard to stick to a timetable travelling that far.'

'There is a little leeway, but the faster you get them to the Border the better.'

Rio nodded slightly, hard eyes fixed on Jugador's face. 'Not all of them are just labourers, are they?'

Jugador's eyes pinched down. 'That is not your concern.'

'The hell it's not. I'm caught with a bunch of peons trying for a bit better life the other side of the Rio and I'm in a lot of trouble. The peons turn out to be political fugitives and I'm in more trouble than I can shake a stick at. And if the *rurales* don't shoot me on the spot, they'll string me up as soon as they find a tree tall enough.'

Jugador stepped closer to the freighter after casting a quick look towards the Mexicans, lowering his voice. 'You take the usual precautions and there will be no trouble. But if you have to take *extra* precautions, then you will do this, too. *Comprende,* Rio?'

In other words, if he had to bribe someone then it would come out of Rio's pocket.

'I need more money, Jug.'

Jugador smiled crookedly. 'It will be taken off your debt, *amigo*. This is the simplest and best way, no?'

'No – I'll still need more *dinero* if I have to pay out bribes on the spot. And they'll be asking for big ones if we're that close to the Border. They'll know we can't take 'em back, can't even try to push 'em across some other place because they'll simply alert the patrols to watch for us – anonymously, naturally.' He shook his head. 'The sons of bitches'll have me over a barrel if they want to shake me down at that stage, Jug – so you come up with some more *dinero* or the deal's off as of now.'

'You do not tell me what you will do, gringo!' the gambler snapped, face darkening. '*I* give the orders!'

'Then make them sensible ones. I'm not riding into a shakedown right on the Border with empty pockets.'

'Take some extra cash with you.' Jugador was indifferent to what he saw as only a slight problem. 'You must have some on hand.'

'That's it, Jugador, I don't have the ready cash to play with.'

The gambler frowned. 'This – *friend*, you take shooting grizzlies, he did not pay you?'

Rio swore softly. 'I lost the money.'

He wasn't surprised when the gambler burst out laughing. The Mexicans in the corner glanced across warily, uncomfortable, no doubt anxious to get away.

'You are a fool, Rio! I have always known it. A big goddamn gringo fool! *You lost it!* Stupid gringo lost it!'

'Not stupid enough to start this deal without a lot more cash in my pocket.' He jerked his head towards the Mexicans. 'If they're all just peons I'm *El Presidente's* boot-licker. You and the *alcalde* are gonna get your fingers burned messing in politics. I want no part of it.'

Jugador grinned, raising one finger. 'You know, I was hoping you would resist, *amigo!* So I take precautions.'

He snapped his fingers and Rio spun around as he heard a shuffling movement

45

behind him in the shadowed freight shed. There was sudden, alarmed chatter from the Mexican group.

But Rio didn't manage to turn completely before something smashed into his lower right leg and he staggered. The club rose and hit his left leg, too, and he sprawled on the ground. Two shadowy shapes moved against the slats of light coming between the sun-warped clapboards of the freight shed and he groped for his six-gun twisting his body painfully – he had fallen on his right side, pinning his gun-rig. His hand hadn't even touched the butt before the first boot took him in the ribs and he rolled away from it with a grunt. The one with the club struck at his shoulder. Luckily it only glanced off the point or he figured his collarbone would have been busted.

But the arm was numbed clear down to his fingernails and he couldn't grip the gun. The club knocked his hat off, stirred his thick brown hair, searing his scalp. He knew then they weren't going to cripple him too much: just give him lots of pain. Well, he had enough of that already!

He rolled swiftly across the straw-littered ground, over and over, too swiftly for the attackers to react, catching them by surprise. Even Jugador himself had to jump back, startled. Rio slammed into the base of the wall and he tried to push upright but his legs were still too numbed and he fell. The attackers stepped in, kicking, the club swinging. He took the blows because he had no choice and then he rolled his body violently against the Mexicans' legs. That they were not expecting and the one with the club yelled something and staggered and stumbled. The other snatched at the wall, failed to find anything to hold on to and staggered right in front of Rio.

The *americano* bared his teeth and rammed the top of his head into the swarthy face. Bone crunched and blood sprayed as the man fell over, groaning, hands going to his shattered face. The one with the club reached for his weapon that he had dropped and Rio launched himself bodily on top of the man, driving the breath out of him. He used his knees on the man's midriff, not getting as much force into the blows as he would have liked. But it stopped the Mexican briefly and Rio snatched a dangling trace chain on a post and pulled himself upright. His legs wanted to fold but they held him long enough to unhook the chain and he swung it in a vicious, whistling arc as the club lifted threateningly.

The chain broke the man's arm and he screamed as the club fell. Rio doubled the chain and slammed its weight across the side of the Mexican's head as he dropped to his knees and spread out, unconscious. Rio spun, hearing the slobbering breathing behind him as the man reached for the gun rammed into his belt.

Rio's chain, wrapped around his left hand, took the Mexican across the throat and he went down, choking and gagging, to his knees. Rio kicked him in the head, started to turn and froze as he felt a gun muzzle pressing into his spine.

Jugador's voice hissed in his ear. 'You are one mean son of a bitch, *amigo,* and you move fast. But not, I think, fast enough to beat my bullet … the chain, Rio!'

Rio let it fall, rubbed at his aching shoulder. He spoke without turning. 'You're going soft, Jugador. Once you'd've tackled me yourself!' Then, pushing it and knowing the chance he took, he snapped his fingers. 'But you *did* take me on, didn't you? That's how come your face is lopsided.'

'Bastard!' hissed Jugador and he hit Rio behind the ear with the gun barrel.

Rio fell against the wall, slipped down to his knees, shaking his head. Jugador's knee took him in the temple and crushed his head against the wall, holding it there as the gambler gritted:

'You will take these men to San Antonio de Bravo, and you will come back here – and do whatever *El Alcalde* or I wish! You *comprende,* Rio?'

The knee pressed harder and he grunted

an affirmative, but the pressure did not ease up. Jugador just leaned closer.

'You are right – there is a *politico* here. This is a test run. If it is successful – and it had better be successful, my friend! – it will prove a very lucrative business indeed. Be smart – do what you are told and your debts will be erased and you can live a fine life in our wonderful country.'

Then he chuckled and twined his fingers in the dazed Rio's hair, flinging the man face-down.

'For just how *long* you will live, of course, could well be a matter of conjecture... But where else can you go, eh? Where else, you gringo son of a bitch?'

His boot drove brutally against Rio's side on the last word.

CHAPTER 4

INFERNO!

Rio had to use two wagons, one the big Conestoga with a special hidden compartment built in, the other a smaller vehicle with false flooring.

Two wagons meant he had to have another driver plus a relief – more men than he normally used on these wetback runs. He would have preferred to make the run alone, especially as there was a political fugitive among them. But the gambler had refused to identify him. The others, Jugador claimed, were genuine wetback peons looking for Paradise north of the Rio Grande.

Rio reserved his opinion on that: usually these fleeing political types had at least one bodyguard close to hand. Although he studied the group closely, he was hard-put to make a selection: he *thought* one man calling himself 'Ortez' might be the *politico* and he *thought* another named 'Pepe' might be the bodyguard the way he stuck close and watched Ortez's every move, but there was no certainty about it. Likely he was better off not knowing, yet at the same time, such knowledge just might come in handy if *rurales* or the Border Patrol happened upon them.

The weather was hot and it was a long, hard trek to San Antonio de Bravo, a grand name for a slapdash village that made a living on the proceeds of whores and gun-runners and anything else that was less than legal and able to be practised in comparative safety this close to the Border.

Crossing the Madres was less of a problem than Rio had figured. This was a country where *bandidos* were rife and he was a mite surprised that there had been no sightings of silent watchers, let alone a confrontation. A little surprised and mighty relieved.

His Mexican hands were nervous, three wetbacks in each wagon. At the first sign of activity anywhere along the trail or in its vicinity, the order was for them to be packed into the secret compartments immediately. In the smaller, old wagon, this was a cramped, slave-trader space between the actual floor and the fake one that held the goods they were carrying as legitimate freight. A man had to wriggle in backwards, using his shoulders, his nose practically touching the splintery boards above him. Then the end was sealed off and more goods stacked in front of it in such a way that they appeared part of the main load.

In the bigger Conestoga, there was a small cube of space, about three feet on a side, right in the midst of the freight goods. The outsides were covered in hessian with padding and even a hole 'worn' in the fabric, allowing part of a carton of safety pins to show. Actually, it was only the labelled part of the original carton, but it looked authentic. It had worked well on several past occasions and no one had yet asked for the 'bale' to be moved. If that day ever came, it would call for some mighty fast talking – or mighty fast something. He had thought about it for a long time before coming up with a solution – drastic but workable.

The hideout was a hell-hole with three men packed inside and only limited air, but wetbacks were prepared to endure absolutely appalling conditions to reach the United States and the chance of a better life. Half of them were worked to death and the rest cheated so it was a long way from Paradise, yet, apparently an improvement on the kind of life they had led under an oppressive regime such as ruled the great country at present. There were stirrings, of course – there hardly seemed to be a few months of stability at a time before someone was claiming to be the new *El Salvador*. Right now it was someone named Juano Leon Estrada – at least that was the name he was using. Some said he was actually a disgruntled member of the current *El*

Presidente's family...

It wouldn't be long before Mexico once again exploded into civil war, Rio figured, and he was wondering just how to meet that problem if and when it arose. *El Alcalde* and Jugador had already hinted that his freight business would be useful in running contraband arms to the rebels that were gathering in the sierras.

Rio didn't aim to get involved in any way, so there were likely some lively times ahead...

'*Señor! Señor!*' called the driver of the smaller wagon, a man named Momo. He was pointing to the hills ahead.

Rio looked for and expected to see dust clouds. What he saw was smoke. A lot of smoke. The timber on those hills was afire – and in this country it was highly unlikely that it was from natural causes.

'Get the peons hidden away!' Rio snapped, slowing his own wagon, turning his head to look inside the canvas canopy where his three wetbacks sprawled amongst the stacked goods. 'Time to climb into the box, *amigos*. Pronto!'

The one he had picked for the *politico*, Ortez, snapped his head up. He was older than the others, grey showing in his drooping moustache and at his temples.

'It is too hot!' he snapped in a tone that told Rio he was used to authority and so strengthening his belief that this man was the most important of the six.

'Hot or not, you get your butt in there, *señor*, or it's gonna be in a sling.'

'My frien' does not unnerstand your stupid Yankee language, *señor!*' This was growled by 'Pepe', the one who was never far from Ortez, and Rio was sure now he had it right – Pepe was Ortez's bodyguard, and doing his job now.

'Then you translate for him, friend, but get the hell into that box.'

Pepe squinted, looking past Rio's shoulder. 'There does not seem to be any danger.'

'There's smoke in the hills. There's been no storm or even lightning. My guess is it's been deliberately lit to make us take the lower trail – and that only leads to a narrow pass where I suspect we might find the men who lit that fire.'

'*Bandidos?*' asked Ortez, who obviously did not need any translation into Spanish.

Rio nodded. 'My guess.'

'It is too early to climb into that wooden oven,' Ortez said, complaining, watching Rio's face steadily.

'They'll be watching through glasses or telescopes as soon as we round that bend in the trail. Now if you want to save your neck, *get in the damn box!*'

Pepe started to rise but Ortez placed a hand on his arm. 'Perhaps our driver is right. It will be uncomfortable, *more* than uncomfortable, but...'

Pepe whirled and took his growing anger out on the silent, rawboned, half-starved genuine wetback who was sitting on a bag of produce, watching the others with worried eyes. Pepe shoved the man roughly until he fell awkwardly amongst other goods and then snarled a curse at the floundering man before helping Rio move some of the goods stacked on top of the fake bale-box.

In minutes the lid was back in place and Rio stacked the other freight on top, lashing it down to make it appear as if it hadn't been disturbed since the wagon had left Sonora.

'OK, Momo?' Rio called across to the small wagon where the Mexican was just closing the tailgate.

'*Sí, señor* ... one is fatter than he looks. Splinters have stuck in the end of his nose.'

Rio nodded, looked at the relief driver. 'You pretend – and I mean *pretend* – to be sleeping amongst the freight but keep a gun handy. We may have to fight. They'll concentrate on the big wagon so as soon as you see or hear me start to shoot, you get your gun working, *comprende?*'

The man grinned with tombstone teeth, nodding, slapping the butt of a revolver rammed into his belt. 'Fighting pay!'

Rio almost smiled. 'Yeah, sure. Extra pay if we have to fight, Emilio.'

But a fight was out of the question when they reached the pass.

There had been no choice but to take the trail through the pass: the fire was well ablaze and the way over the hills was impossible, so the wagons reluctantly headed for the pass. Rio had seen the sun flashing off lenses amongst the boulders but he wasn't prepared for the bunch of riders that suddenly appeared, blocking the narrow pass.

Or the even bigger bunch that blocked the only way of retreat.

Rio swore under his breath: there were bandits here, but there were *rurales* as well. And that was a combination that set his teeth on edge. They seldom worked together; in fact there was a traditional enmity between the two. But if there had been enough money spread around in the right places on both sides, an alliance was not unknown.

And usually it ended in wholesale slaughter.

A lieutenant of the *rurales* was the spokesman, sided by a mean-eyed, big-nosed bandit that he figured must be the ruthless killer the Mexicans called *Nariz Grande*: Bignose, a man who enjoyed killing and hated gringos.

The *teniente,* yellow-faced, his uniform grubby and carelessly worn, tapped his quirt against the top of his scuffed leather half-boot.

'My men will unload your wagons, *señor.*'

'No need for that, *teniente,*' said Rio, keeping his tone reasonable and without any trace of alarm – he hoped. 'I have men who are expert at handling such freight – and stowing it again correctly.'

The lieutenant smiled thinly. 'There will be no need for stowing it, *amigo.* We are relieving you of your load. We have mules waiting – they can handle the mountain trails more easily than your cumbersome wagons. In any case, my men enjoy watching wagons burn.'

'Hey, *teniente*' There was alarm in Rio's voice now. 'Let us brew some fresh coffee and discuss this matter – I am sure we can reach an amicable arrangement.'

The lieutenant slid his gaze to Bignose and almost too fast for Rio to see, the man's six-gun came up and fired twice. Momo's skinny figure was hurled from the driving seat of the small wagon and before it had hit the ground, Emilio rose from his faked sleep, bringing up his pistol and firing wildly.

A dozen guns crashed from the group and Emilio jerked and flailed as he was punched off the load to hit the ground, flopping in the dust.

The lieutenant hadn't touched his gun, but he pointed his quirt at Rio whose six-gun was almost free of leather and shook his head slowly. Looking down the smoking muzzles of a dozen rifles and the rising, cocked revolver in Bignose's right hand, Rio sighed and released his gun butt, the Colt slipping back into the holster. The *teniente* smiled and started to speak but stopped when there came cries of alarm from the smaller wagon.

The wetbacks had panicked and were

screaming to be let out.

The *rurale* officer swivelled his gaze to Rio and shook his head sadly, then looked at Bignose.

'Our information was correct, *amigo*. Some of this freight is alive – for now.'

'*Teniente*,' Rio said quickly. 'They're only wetbacks, looking to improve their lives a little. Perhaps you could spare them, offer them places amongst your men.' He gestured to the motley groups of bandits and rural soldiers.

The lieutenant pretended to give the matter some thought, even discussed it at length with Bignose who was for shooting them immediately, but Rio knew the man was only amusing himself: he had no intention of letting the wetbacks live.

Nor Rio himself.

He snapped orders and men started unloading the wagons. The wetbacks in the smaller wagon were still crying for mercy, and to be released from their hiding place, but their pleas fell on deaf ears.

The men hidden in Rio's wagon made no sound. He wondered about the skinny wetback, surmised that Ortez's self-styled bodyguard had silenced the man.

But it did no good. The lieutenant and his men made a big deal about finding what appeared to be a bale of goods firmly attached to the wagonbed. The men unloading sweated and strained and were told by Bignose to leave it be.

They clambered down hurriedly when the bandit lit the stub of a cigarillo between his fat lips, then flicked the still burning vesta into the wagonbed, against the outer covering of the fake bale.

Rio started forward, stopped dead when a gun muzzle rammed into his midriff. 'You sadistic bastards!' he yelled as Bignose moved to the smaller wagon and set fire to the canopy. The screams of the trapped wetbacks rose louder than ever.

Closer, the men caught in the inferno of the wagonbox began yelling and soon the sound changed to choking screams and Rio moved away from the stench of burning flesh. Bignose's face was intent as he stared into the flames, listening to the death screams of the wetbacks. The others seemed to be enjoying the infernos, too, and those who weren't were pawing over the goods, breaking open packages and bales and boxes, looting what they could while their officer was watching the fires.

Almost every man there was either fire-watching or looting. There was one beside Rio who was obviously eager to join the looters, the rifle he had been using to cover Rio sagging unheeded now. Rio knew this was the time to make a break if ever he was going to...

For underneath both hiding places in the wagons were secreted several sticks of dynamite complete with fuses and detonators. He had found the hiding places of use on other occasions and had blasted his way out of trouble twice before with such precautions. A mite hard on the wagons, though.

There was no chance of getting to them

now, of course, and putting them to use. But the fire would be eating through the hardwood planks by now, the short fuses hissing and writhing with the dead wetbacks' contorted bodies lying on the planks above...

He swung an elbow into the man supposed to be guarding him, snatched his rifle, clubbed him with the butt. Then, as he turned the gun on the lieutenant and Bignose, the smaller wagon exploded.

It went with a shattering, flaming roar. The wetbacks' bodies were hurled into the air together with planks and iron-wheel rims and a thundering blast wave that cut down soldiers and bandits like a scythe through ripe wheat.

Rio was already running, doubled over, but even so the second blast wave caught him and hurled him end over end off the edge of the trail. He hit the softer earth of the slope and began to slide and roll, almost deafened, catching glimpses of body parts scattering across the sky together with splintered timbers. Some of the team horses were screaming and down. Most of the bandits and soldiers were unhorsed or writhing on the ground.

But Rio didn't know that right then. He was still sliding and then he crashed into a tree stump and he knew nothing at all as roaring blackness overtook him.

CHAPTER 5

FAST GUNS

There were some who survived the blast. Some *rurales* and some *bandidos*. Not many, and they were dazed, wounded and partially deafened.

They looked around cursorily, thinking of their own skins, wanting to get out of this neck of the woods, believing that the explosions might bring other *rurales* who were not in the pay of Bignose. The bandit chief himself had escaped with his life, although he had a chest wound from a jagged splinter torn from the Conestoga. He was barely conscious and his men got him away roped to a horse. Other shocked and still frightened horses ran free. The surviving *rurales* rode off with the bandits.

They had looked for Rio's body, and one of them had seen it sprawled at the bottom of the slope, looking lifeless. He had lifted his rifle, planning on putting a couple of bullets into Rio to make sure, but one of his companions had stayed him.

'No more noise, *amigo*. We should vamoose pronto.'

The man with the rifle thought that was good advice, spat in the general direction of Rio's body and joined his *compadres* as they rode back deeper into the hills.

They had been gone a good half-hour before Rio came round, head ringing, hearing dulled, body sore and clothes torn. He sat up and looked around him, bewildered at first, until he remembered and then knew why he couldn't hear well. He had a stomach-churning moment when he wondered if he would always be this deaf now, but figured there was nothing he could do about it.

What he had to do now was get out of here.

And quickly.

That presented no problems, as it happened. He easily caught one of the riderless horses, took an undamaged, though scratched, Winchester from a bandit's broken body and mounted awkwardly. He had to grab tightly to the saddlehorn, swaying and disoriented as dizziness flooded over him. He knew this was most likely associated with his blast-damaged ears and made his movements slow and easy. Several times he almost fell out of the saddle as he rode away from the scene of carnage and devastation.

He was closer to San Antonio de Bravo than he was to the Sonora line and decided to ride there. The man he was supposed to meet would be waiting for the wetbacks, anyway, and he reckoned he owed him some kind of explanation.

Rio arrived in Bravo just before noon the next day. His hearing was improving, though not yet back to normal. The dizziness was decreasing but occasionally caught him unawares and made him stagger and weave as if he was drunk.

That was how he entered the Cantina Rosario, clinging to the batwings for a few moments to steady himself. Some of the drinkers laughed, all of them watched him as he weaved his unsteady way to the bar and ordered tequila. The sweating barman eyed him suspiciously, lifted a hand and rubbed fingers and thumb together: apparently he figured a man who looked as dishevelled as Rio would not have the price of a drink.

Rio slapped a silver dollar on the bar top and the barkeep poured him a shotglass of raw liquid fire without expression. Rio downed it and, unable to speak because of the searing pain that suddenly grasped his throat, indicated that he wanted another drink.

He was sipping this when a man who looked like a half-breed approached. Tall, slim, almost hipless, and wearing twin guns in a Border *buscadero* rig. He was about Rio's age and he thumbed back his hat, leaned on the bar, snapped his fingers and when the 'keep set down a shotglass in front of him, filled it from Rio's bottle. He flashed white teeth as he lifted the glass towards his mouth.

'You do not mind, of course, *señor.*'

'Of course not – long as you don't mind having that glass smashed through your teeth if you try to drink from it.'

The 'breed's smile disappeared and he froze with the rim of the glass almost touching his mouth. His eyes had gone small and hard and dangerous. He did not lower the glass and spoke very quietly.

'You do not speak to me like that – gringo.'

He made the name an insult and Rio said without any expression at all, 'Why not – 'breed?'

Men moved away, clearing a space at the bar. The 'breed laughed after a pause and then shrugged. But while his right hand was still holding the glass close to his mouth, his left blurred down to his gun butt and whipped the revolver clear of leather.

Rio's Colt blasted and the man gasped in shock, staggered and clasped his left leg, which didn't seem to be able to support him any longer. The gun thudded to the floor and the 'breed sagged down to one knee, gritting his teeth and making animal noises with the pain.

Rio waved the gunsmoke away from in front of his face. 'Take it easy, you'll live. Likely won't even have a limp in a couple of months.'

'I – *kill* – you!' the 'breed gritted.

'Not today, Luis.'

The wounded man, sitting now with his back to the bar as the drinkers slowly resumed their places, snapped his head up as he tore off a kerchief and wrapped it tightly around his left thigh.

'You know me?'

'Sure – Luis Banda. You never were as fast as you figured, Luis.'

Banda squinted up at Rio. 'I – don't – recall – you.'

Rio was actually cursing himself for slipping up that way: he should never have mentioned the man's name. 'Oh, I've seen you round the Border towns the last couple of years, notching up those fancy guns, killing has-beens or kids strutting like a fighting cock, but never taking on any real talent. You have a lousy reputation, Luis.'

Knotting the kerchief, Luis said with a snarl, 'Like you, mebbe?'

'Yeah, maybe like me. They call me Rio.'

Banda swore. 'I knew you were the one when I entered! I am supposed to meet you, for–' he lowered his voice here '–Mr Barnaby.'

Rio arched his eyebrows. Then he smiled slowly. 'Well, well, well – *Mister* Barnaby, the bigshot Texan owner of B Bar B don't mind using a little wetback labour, huh?'

Luis Banda hissed through his teeth. '*Silencio!* You do not bandy that name around in connection with *peones!*'

'They weren't all *peones*, Luis,' Rio said quietly and at the man's curious look, picked up the tequila bottle and glasses and walked towards a table. It was occupied by three locals who glanced at each other and then rose as one, leaving the table for Rio. He nodded his thanks as they edged away, toed out a chair and dropped into it. 'Come and join me, Luis. We've got a little talking to do...'

Banda looked savagely at the seated Rio and reached out a hand. 'Help me, damn you!'

'You can make it,' Rio said casually, sipping a drink. He poured the second glass full. 'C'mon – a couple of these'll do you good.'

The room fell silent as Banda glared for a long minute and then began to slide and hitch his way across to the table on his buttocks, wounded leg thrust out ahead of him. Close to the table, he reached a hand up towards Rio but the gringo shook his head.

'If I wanted to help you I wouldn't've shot you in the first place. You're lucky, Luis. I could've killed you.'

Banda tried to keep the snarling look of

malevolence on his face, but it was plain for anyone to see that he realized that Rio spoke the truth: he was lucky to be alive.

He struggled and heaved and grunted, getting an elbow on to a chair and straining to lift himself high enough so that he could twist and sit in it. He was gasping, sweating with the effort. People were looking at him – or looking towards the table. Many of the stares were directed at Rio who seemed oblivious or totally indifferent about it all.

He pushed the glass towards Luis Banda who tossed the strong liquor down and held out the glass again. Rio filled it and his own.

'Barnaby sent you down to meet me?'

'Din' know who I was to meet, just a gringo bringin' in a bunch of wetbacks.'

'And you picked me out of the crowd.'

'You were the only gringo and you looked like you had travelled far – and you are a day late.'

'Tell you why.' And Rio told him, watching Luis's pain-filled eyes widen.

'*Dios!* You killed Bignose?'

Rio shook his head. 'I dunno. Think he might've lived. Didn't see his body but then some of them...' He grimaced and shrugged.

'Just who are you?' Luis asked in a hushed voice, frowning as he stared hard into Rio's face. 'I think maybe I should know you, gringo.'

Rio's eyes narrowed. 'Better if you don't. Savvy?'

Luis seemed as if he would retort sharply, but something in Rio's manner and those penetrating eyes drained the blood from his face and he fidgeted with his glass, spilling some of the liquor.

'Well – I *don't* know you. It's just that a man so fast – he must have some sort of reputation along the Border, eh? Or in the States, maybe...?'

'Luis, don't make me sorry I didn't put that bullet through your black heart.'

'OK, OK!' the 'breed said quickly. 'But you and me – will meet again one day, eh? And maybe I will be faster.'

Rio spread his hands. 'Only one way to

find out that, Luis. And, remember, there's no second place.'

As soon as Barnaby saw Luis Banda drive the buckboard into his ranchyard he knew something was wrong. When he had sent the man down to San Antonio de Bravo to meet the delivery of wetbacks before heading into Sonora to investigate this Rio son of a bitch, Banda had been forking a palomino that he boasted he had taken from a gunfighter up in Santa Fe.

''Course I had to pry the reins from his poor dead fingers,' Luis had joked. 'But the horse is mine and I will kill it rather than have anyone else even think about riding it, let alone try to take it from me.'

When the buckboard came to a stop in a cloud of dust, no palomino hitched to the tailgate, Kelly Treece came to the door of the barn where he had been working, greasing axle hubs on a chuckwagon. He watched with curiosity as Banda struggled down out of the seat, reached into the buckboard and brought out a pair of crutches. Luis tucked them under his arms and made his way to the porch where Barnaby sat in a cane chair, smoking a hand-made cherrywood pipe. The rancher's cold eyes followed Banda's progress as he struggled up the few steps onto the porch and leaned the crutches against the wall as he slid down into a chair next to Barnaby.

'What happened?' the rancher asked harshly.

'Wetbacks are gone – Bignose and his bandits tried to take 'em and this Rio blew up his wagons. Not sure if he killed Bignose or not, but wiped out half his gang.'

'He blew up my wetbacks!' Barnaby gritted.

Luis tried to explain how it was, putting Rio in as bad a light as possible.

Barnaby swore. 'I went down there to arrange that shipment personally – there was a very important man amongst those wetbacks. I didn't know this Rio was going to be involved. Now he's killed them all!' He thumped his knee with a fist. 'Christ! D'you know the trouble he's caused?'

'Mighty tough man, Mister Barnaby.'

'I know! I've dealt with the son of a bitch!' Barnaby growled. 'He's a dead man walkin' now! You find out anything about him?'

Luis had been saving this, getting the bad news out of the way first, knowing – hoping – that what he had to tell Barnaby next would blunt the man's anger at him.

'I thought it best to come straight back and tell you about the wetbacks, Mister Barnaby.'

That cut no ice with the rancher. 'In other words, you know nothing!'

'He outdrew me in a *cantina* in Bravo,' Luis admitted slowly, indicating his bandaged thigh. 'Man that fast has to be known somewheres. I got to thinkin' and it came to me just as I crossed the Border back into Texas. He's a man name of Brent Rivers – guess that's how come he picked 'Rio' as a name to go by.'

'Seems I've heard of this Brent Rivers,'

Barnaby said slowly 'but can't place him…'

'No, he's not from Texas. Stampin' ground's up north, Nebraska and the Dakotas. Fastest man with a gun ever to bust a cap, they say. Got tired of every two-bit drifter callin' him out, so went to Wyoming, tried to shake his rep by workin' the ranches. He was doin' all right on a big spread owned by a man named Zachary Holt–'

'Now that's a name I do know! Biggest cattleman in the north. He doesn't just run a ranch, he runs an empire. Fighting to have Wyoming admitted to the Union as a State.'

Banda nodded. 'That's him – had three sons. Doted on the young one, Tyler. Kid was always in trouble, and the other two brothers, Kyle and Zack Junior, had to haul him outta scrapes all the time. But when he was loco enough to call out Brent Rivers, they was away on round-up and so was the old man. Rivers killed Tyler in a shoot-out and when he tried to explain to Zachary the old man grabbed his shotgun and Rivers shot him, too. Din' kill him, but crippled him up some so's he can't walk without a stick and can hardly sit a hoss.'

'This Rivers sounds like a real cold-blooded killer.'

Was there a trace of worry now in Barnaby's voice? wondered Luis Banda. But he merely shrugged. 'He left a lot of dead men up north, and when Zack sent Junior and Kyle after him they were found dead.'

'Jesus!'

Barnaby was impressed despite himself. At the same time, a little shiver of fear tingled through his body.'

God almighty! He had drawn a gun on this Rio!

Sweat started to prickle his face and trickled down inside his collar. He swallowed, knowing he was a mighty lucky man to be still alive...

All of which did little or nothing to lessen the hatred he felt for the man who called himself Rio.

He had humiliated Barnaby – *Mister* Barnaby – hadn't even used the term out of courtesy! Now the son of a bitch would pay – one way or another. And anything Luis Banda could tell him would be by way of a bonus.

You could never know too much about men like Rio.

Banda continued, quietly, confidently, sure he had Barnaby's full attention now. And that meant the possibility of higher pay.

'Old Zack went plumb loco, they say. He swore out warrants agin Rivers, called in a lotta favours amongst lawmen and other ranchers up there, politicians, anyone who could help him track down Rivers – who just disappeared. So old Zack made sure he'd never be able to come back to the States. Kept gettin' them warrants renewed, chargin' Rivers with the murder of young Tyler – and put up a standin' reward for the man who brought him Rivers' head,' He paused, then said almost reverently. 'Ten thousand bucks.'

Barnaby stiffened. 'My God, that's a fortune by any standard. I'd heard rumours that Rio was on the run, and there were bounty hunters after him, but I didn't know the story. You're sure about this, Luis?'

Banda wasn't *certain* sure Rio was this Brent Rivers, but he nodded without hesitation. 'He's the man, Mister Barnaby. He's the man...'

Barnaby sat back in his chair and smiled slowly. His pipe had gone out but that didn't seem to worry him at all.

He had other things on his mind, now, heart hammering and his belly churning wildly.

CHAPTER 6

AVENGER

'You let the *peones* burn and then blew them up!'

The *alcalde* almost screamed the words, his eyes bulging as he stared hard at the relaxed, though battered Rio.

'There was nothing I could do to save them after Bignose set fire to the wagons,' Rio told him patiently. 'They were already dead as far as anyone was concerned. It just so happened that I had some dynamite hidden under the frame of the bed on each wagon. I'd had trouble before with *bandidos* on the freight run and twice I was able to get away by using dynamite. So I had some already rigged in case it might come in handy again…' He shrugged. 'There was no chance to stop the fuses catching alight so...' He spread his hands and made a subdued *boom!* with his lips.

The mayor's eyes seemed to bulge even more. 'Do you realize what you have done?' Rio shook his head, then said, 'Well, maybe I've got some notion. That *hombre* calling himself "Ortez" – he looked too well-fed and sure of himself to be a peon. The one with him could've been a bodyguard.'

'You have eyes that are too sharp, amigo,' said Jugador from his desk chair. The meeting was in the gambler's office on the top floor of his *cantina*. 'They will get you into a lot more trouble than you are in now if you do not take care.'

Rio smiled thinly. 'More trouble, Jugador? Listen, I lost two good drivers, two good wagons I have no idea how I'm going to replace. I shot a man in Bravo and was plain damn lucky that the resident *Tenient Rurale* was out on Border patrol at the time. I have Luis Banda after me and...'

Both men stiffened. The mayor asked,

hesitantly, 'What has Luis Banda to do with this?'

'Oh, didn't I tell you – he's the one Barnaby sent down to Bravo to pick up his wetbacks.'

They exchanged glances and Jugador's mouth worked in a silent curse.

'That one is dangerous – a pity you didn't shoot him, Rio.' The man smirked, being smart.

'I did – in the leg.'

They stared. Silence for a long minute.

'You outdrew Luis Banda?' hissed the *alcalde*.

'Uh-huh.'

'Then if it is true, you are the fastest gun alive!' There was undisguised admiration in Jugador's words.

Rio had nothing to say to that. Both men began to look a little worried, perhaps realizing finally just who they had been dealing with these last couple of years, blackmailing Rio all this time into doing what they wanted. There was sweat on their brows: he must have gone along with it simply because it suited him. A man like Rio could have killed them both between draws on his cigarette...

Any time he felt like it.

They both felt a little sick and the mayor ran a tongue over dry lips.

'We have co-operated well,' the *alcalde* said, pausing to clear his throat, forcing a smile that looked kind of weak and trembling. 'I mean – it has been to our mutual advantage and–'

'Hogwash,' cut in Rio. 'It's been to your advantage. But I've let it be because it suited me and I knew you two snakes wouldn't want to kill off the goose that was laying so many golden eggs for you.' He held up a hand as they both started to protest. 'Forget it. You're slime, both of you, and I don't give a good goddamn for either of you. But this has suited me fine, this cover, and I've been getting some genuine freight custom. And you can relax. I'll pay my debts and I won't kill you – for now. But things are gonna operate kind of differently, you *comprende?*'

'Of course, of course, Rio, *amigo!*' the mayor said with that same trembling smile, dark wet patches showing under his arms on his silk shirt and where it stretched tight across his ample midriff. 'Two years we have – er – cared for you and that must be long enough now, eh?'

Jugador remained silent but he shot his pardner a cold look.

'No it's not,' Rio said. 'You don't know all the details of why I'm hiding here and I don't aim to tell you. I'll stay put for now and you two are gonna be even more generous than you have been.'

The mayor winced: he knew just how 'generous' they had been, charging exorbit-ant rates of interest on money Rio had been coerced into borrowing from them, using their knowledge that he was a fugitive to force him to do what they wanted. He still felt sick when thinking how he could now be dead if Rio had chosen to rebel...

'How – generous?' Jugador asked quietly,

the thought of paying out money overriding even his newly acquired fear of this Rio. He had known all along it was risky, but Rio's apparent ease of cooperation had lulled him into a false sense of security. Like the mayor, he, too, realized he was lucky to be still alive.

'Well, like I said, I'll need two new wagons. I'll have to hire replacement drivers and I think I'll drop out of the wetback smuggling game.'

'No!' snapped Jugador. 'With the unrest in the south, that business is booming and we can make a lot of money.' He smiled quickly. '*All* of us can make a lot of money, Rio, *amigo!*'

'Nice of you to include me in the profit, Jug, but I'm not interested. Get someone else.'

'But – but it is *perfecto!* Your wagons, they travel all over, north to the Border, south to the country where men are wishing to flee to the *Estados Unidos* – whole families in some cases. There is much *dinero* to be made, Rio!'

'Then you make it – count me out of that

side of it. I'm not getting mixed up in anyone's politics.'

The mayor cut in with his arguments, but Jugador sensed that Rio was showing a stubborn side to him they hadn't seen before.

'I – think we have to look for a new man, *alcalde*,' he said quietly and his words brought a deep frown to the mayor's face.

'*Aiiyyee!* This is indeed a very bad day! Rio, *compadre* – you will not reconsider?'

Rio shook his head and the mayor sighed heavily, spread his hands helplessly, looking at Jugador.

'You will have to – enlist someone, Jugador. Perhaps from your card tables…?'

The gambler made no sign he had even heard, but Rio knew what the *alcalde* meant. Jugador would play with a fixed deck, drive some poor son of a bitch who could help them into a debt he would have no hope of paying back – then show him an easy way out. Smuggle wetbacks or guns or even drugs where and when they wished and his debt would dwindle at alarming speed – except that the actual 'speed' would be more like slow motion. But they would recruit their man and hold him in their power. Rio knew from experience how easily it worked.

'Now, gents – about these wagons,' he said flatly.

It was two weeks before the first wagon was ready, except for painting and some washers for the brake assembly. It was a small vehicle but would be useful on local runs.

By that time, Zutano and Monk were back from their southern deliveries and both men confirmed that things were very edgy down that way, particularly out towards Mexico City where the president was growing more and more brutal as a building rebel force gained more and more supporters.

'Gonna be hell to pay down there mighty soon, I reckon, Rio,' said Zutano. He seemed to have more grey hair showing than Rio remembered, but he knew this wasn't likely. The walnut-wrinkled face, dark and leathery, looked just the same, a lantern jaw jutting aggressively. The pale eyes that had seen so many distant horizons coming closer and closer over the years were still steady and level. 'We had a lot of offers of big money from folk who wanted to get up this way in a hurry.'

'Just offers?'

Zutano shrugged. 'Some of them poor devils I'd've carried for nothin' – and I tell you I come close to it a couple times – but we refused. As usual.'

Zutano had always been inclined to see where good profit could be made on the return run north by including a few desperate peons or political fugitives. *Soft-hearted...* Rio shook his head: he had so far not fallen foul of the *real* authorities and he didn't aim to now that he had laid things on the line with the mayor and Jugador.

'None of our business, Zutano,' Rio said flatly, and included Monje, or 'Monk' as he was known – in his gaze.

Monk was a blocky, well-muscled Mexican, hard-working, tough as nails, and loyal to Rio although he had not known the man until he had come down across the Border from the *Estados Unidos* a couple of years back.

'You aim to buy into this trouble that's a'brewing, Monk?'

Monk pursed his lips. 'It is my country, Rio, but I have no *relaciones* or family in the south. And I still work for you.'

Rio nodded 'Good enough. You still work for me, Zutano?'

The man spat. 'No need for you to ask that!'

'My apologies. Start painting that wagon while I make up the harness. Sooner we get it on the trail loaded with freight the better. The books ain't lookin' good, friend.'

Monk left but Zutano hesitated and Rio frowned as he saw how uncomfortable the man was. 'What?' he asked.

Zutano scratched at the stubble on his heavy jaw. 'You know them folk I said offered good money to be brought north…?'

Rio stiffened and his eyes narrowed. 'Go on.'

Zutano sighed. 'Well, there was this woman – young, beautiful woman...'

'Hundreds of 'em down here – but what about her?'

'Calls herself Rosita de Ayora. Comes from a good family. Well, she's got a brother up this way, at Los Hoyos. He's poorly and the stage was out of commission because of bandit raids and–'

Rio sighed. 'Where is she now?'

Zutano stared a moment, then forced a grin, jerking a thumb over his right shoulder. 'Waitin' in the small store shed. She was wonderin' if you – we – could help her get the rest of the way.'

'Seems we've already helped her. There's a stage leaves tomorrow around noon.'

'Well, she wants to get to him as fast as she can, and I sort of – suggested – we might be able to let her have a horse and some grub to see her through...'

Rio shook his head sadly. 'How old are

you, Zutano?'

'Don't rightly know, mebbe fifty.'

'Mebbe *sixty!* And your head is still turned by a pretty face and a smile…'

'Aw, Rio, this kid's genuine! She's all upset and, well, it was kinda embarrassin' seein' all them tears…'

'Bring her up,' Rio said resignedly, as he went behind his desk and dropped wearily into his chair, thumbing back his weathered hat.

Zutano was back in minutes and Rio first laid eyes on Rosita de Ayora. She was in her very early twenties, he figured, had smooth golden skin, flashing eyes, a head of thick raven curls and a pouting mouth that made him uncomfortable.

'*Señorita,*' he said with a slight bow, Zutano smiling beamingly to one side. 'My man there tells me you need a horse.'

'To see my sick brother, *señor* – I can pay.' Her white teeth tugged at her full lower lip and there came a sadness in her dark eyes. 'I – I fear he may not last much longer.'

'What's wrong with him?' Rio asked.

'Fever – the swamps, you know. Many men get fever up there.'

'But those are peons, doing the hard work no one else wants – for low pay. Surely a brother of yours...?' He let the question hang and she frowned slightly.

'Oh! You mean because we come from a good family? *Sí*, but Rodolfo was always the – how you say it? The wild cattle...?' She glanced at Zutano and he cleared his throat hurriedly.

'You mean "maverick", *señorita*...?'

'*Sí!* The maverick! Rodolfo is always the maverick in our family... Señor Rio, we have all heard you are *sympatico* to Mexicans and this is *muy importante* that I reach my brother as soon as possible.' She paused and sniffled, producing a small kerchief from a sleeve and dabbing at her nostrils and eyes. 'Our father died recently and–'

'Aw, Rosita, I never knew that!' Zutano said, full of sympathy. He moved to put an arm about the girl's shaking shoulders as she dug deeper into her drawstring bag, possibly for a larger kerchief.

But she suddenly twisted away, thrusting Zutano hard so that he staggered back, hit a chair and flailed in an effort to stay on his feet.

And when she spun towards the now standing Rio, she had a small pistol held in both hands, the drawstring bag crumpled at her feet.

Her teeth were bared and her knuckles white where she held the gun, the hammer cocking under her thumb. Rio was frozen and then gathered himself to make his move, a dive for the floor.

He was too late.

The shot crashed in the small cluttered office and he was flung back against the wall before sliding down to the floor in a heap.

The girl fumbled to cock the gun for a second shot.

CHAPTER 7

LA SEÑORITA

Zutano was sprawled on the floor, momentarily frozen by the sound of the gunfire. But when he heard also the ratcheting back of the hammer for the second shot, he came to life like a mustang raked with guthook spurs.

He kicked out at the overturned chair and it skidded violently across the floor and crashed into the back of the girl's legs. Her cry of shock and alarm was drowned out by the second shot – this time the bullet went high and punched into the adobe wall, showering dust. As she fell, not quite going down all the way, she swung the smoking pistol towards Zutano who was moving mighty fast for an oldster who often complained of rheumatics knotting up his joints.

His body cannoned into her and she cried out – more in rage than hurt – and he forced her back, threw his weight on her and grappled for that gun hand. He felt a slim wrist, lifted the arm and banged it down against the floor. She cried out with the pain in her knuckles and the gun fell from her grasp. She squirmed out from under and lunged at him, teeth bared and fingers hooked, the nails ready to tear out his throat or his eyes, whichever she could reach. Zutano figured that was enough and she was more than a handful. So he rammed the top of his head up under her small jaw and heard her teeth click together as her head snapped back.

Her eyes rolled and, dazed, she groped for support. He fisted up a handful of hair, slammed her face down on the floor and knelt with one knee between her shoulder blades. Monk burst in, scooped up the fallen pistol. Zutano stood stiffly keeping one boot on the girl's back.

Rio was huddled awkwardly against the base of the wall and even as Zutano opened his mouth to call his name, the freighter gave a half-moan, shook his head and gagged a little as he struggled to sit up. He coughed and winced, a hand clawing into his chest.

'Judas! Where's the blood?' asked the startled Zutano. Monk looked surprised, also.

Rio fumbled in his waistcoat pocket, found only bullet-torn cloth, and then pulled out one side of the vest and reached into the inside pocket. He winced again as he brought out a mangled packet of iron washers, each a couple of inches in diameter. The washers for the new wagon's brake bar...

'Manuel asked me to pick these up – he's putting the finishing touches to the hardware on the new wagon.' Rio looked inside his shirt. 'Man, have I got a bruise coming!'

'Better than a hole lettin' air into your

lung,' opined Zutano, easing his boot off the girl now.

'Who the hell is she?' demanded Rio, standing gingerly, still rubbing at his aching chest. He sat down, watching the girl sit up slowly, blinking.

Zutano shrugged. 'All I know is what I told you.'

She glared at Rio. 'I wanted to kill you! And I will. I can wait!'

'I've never seen you before,' Rio said slowly.

Her eyes were dark and mean, but there was something tempering the meanness. Rio thought, with surprise, that it might even be a touch of sadness.

'You do not know me – but you knew my father.'

He shook his head. 'I never knew anyone named Ayora.'

'But you knew a man calling himself Ortez!'

'The wetback who wasn't really a wetback ... I had him down as a *politico* on the run.'

101

'And you killed him! You blew him to bits!' she sobbed.

'Nothing I could do about it, *señorita* ... Bignose set fire to the wagon and I had it rigged with dynamite.'

She curled a lip. 'You had time to save your own skin!'

He arched his eyebrows. 'What'd you expect me to do? Stand there and let myself be blown to hell?'

'You murdered my father and I will avenge him, gringo! D'you hear me?'

Rio glanced at Zutano. 'What d'we do with her?'

The old man had no answer and Monk made it clear it was no use asking him.

Then the girl's next words got their attention.

'You had better kill me now if you want to live!' She got to her feet, roughly shaking off Monk's helping hand. 'Because I will never give up until you are dead, Rio!'

He sighed. 'Listen – *listen*, damn you! Now just forget the cussing and name-calling. I'll tell you what happened–'

'I am not interested in your explanations!'

Rio sighed heavily, shook his head, clasped his hands together and then released one to rub at the spreading bruise on his chest under his shirt. He looked hard at the girl and she frowned, a little disconcerted, but her jaw jutted defiantly. Then he turned his gaze to Monk and Zutano.

'All right – she's going to be a goddamned heap of trouble. She's too stupid to listen, and she's gonna bust a gut trying to kill me.' He jerked his head towards the door. 'Take her down by the tar pit where we dump the old wagon parts. Shoot her and toss her body in – it'll sink and she'll never be found.'

There was profound silence in the hot office as he swung his boots up on to a half-open desk drawer, took out a cigarillo and lit up. He frowned as he shook out the match, ignoring the girl who was now white-faced, looked at his two men.

'Well, what the hell're you waiting for? You

know it's the best way – the only way.'

He stared hard at Zutano who suddenly lost his blank look and nodded, turning to Monk. 'Yeah, Rio's right, Monk. She'll be in our hair all the time otherwise. No one'll find her in that tar pit – she'll be just another lost *señorita* an' there's hundreds of them. Let's go, miss.'

He tugged at her arm but she fought him, and there was fear streaking her face as she grabbed the edge of Rio's desk and thrust her face towards him.

'You would do this, wouldn't you!' There was a tremor in her voice although she tried to disguise it with anger. 'You would have me murdered and my body hidden. Well, it is as Zutano said: the best way if you wish to go on living – *pig!* I will die without avenging my father, but I curse you and your children and their children! D'you hear me, *pig?* A black curse on you and your family for all eternity! I only regret that I will not be here to see it destroy you!'

Rio exhaled a long stream of smoke, not

taking his eyes of her pinched, ghost-like features.

'You are a damn little hothead, ain't you?' Rio shifted in his seat, signed to Monk who started to pull Rosita back from the desk. 'And you sure hate mighty hard. If you love the same way some lucky *hombre* who doesn't know it yet is gonna have one helluva grand life ahead of him. It'll be lively, damned lively, but all that making up afterwards will make it all worth while.'

She frowned, staring. 'Who are you to predict my life for me? You are going to have me killed, anyway, so you contradict yourself, pig!'

'Ease up on that *puerco, señorita, por favor,* if you don't mind. No, I'm not going to have you killed, for Chris'sakes. But you are gonna sit there and listen to me explain how things happened when your father died. And, by the way, if he wanted my help, he should've asked for it.'

'You lie! He did ask for it! He said he would ask as soon as he met you!'

'Well, thing is, Rosita, we never met. The men who arranged the whole deal had the wetbacks all lined up in my barn and we got away fast. Along the way, your father never even spoke to me. No! Don't bother calling me a liar. It's true – all that I'm telling you is true. You believe it – or don't – as you like, but I swear it is the truth.'

'Rio ain't one to lie, miss,' Zutano said quietly but she only continued to stare coldly at the freighter.

He went on and told her about the hold-up in the narrow pass in Chihuahua and how Bignose had deliberately fired the wagons after stealing the goods.

'They'd already shot up the hiding places where the wet backs were,' Rio concluded quietly, to make it a little easier on her feelings. 'I'd say your father and the others were dead from gunshot wounds before the dynamite exploded … I'm sorry, but there wasn't one damn thing I could've done.'

She was sitting in a chair by this time, her lower lip trembling, the jaw, too. Her eyes glistened. 'It was still your fault!' she choked only half aloud.

'No – I didn't even want to be there. I'm not interested in running wetbacks across the Border and I sure don't aim to touch anything political. I need to stay down here, *señorita,* and the men who made the arrangements know this and so can make me do what they want – or they could. Things have changed just recently and I've got more to say in the matter now.' He stood, walked around the desk to her chair. 'I dunno what I'm going to do with you, Rosita. I savvy how you feel and you've got plenty of guts. I guess if you try again to kill me, I'm just gonna have to shoot back.'

'You would – shoot a woman?' she sounded genuinely shocked. 'But of course you would, pi– I think so, anyway.'

'Well, you think about it. We've got plenty of work to do here.' Rio held out his hand and Zutano handed him the gun. 'You and Monk get that wagon painted – and take Manuel what's left of his bag of washers.

Tell him to save me the bent ones. I might have 'em framed.'

The men left and she watched him warily now that they were alone. He hefted the gun, not looking at it, leaned his shoulders against the wall.

'I'd better keep this for now.'

She almost smiled. 'I have a knife.'

'Yeah, I guess you'll find something if you plan to make another try to kill me. You don't believe me, eh?'

She hesitated. 'D'you know a man named Morelos? Antonio Morelos?'

'I once knew a Tony Morell who told me his real name was Morelos,' Rio said carefully.

She nodded. '*Sí*, that is him. He is a gunrunner.'

Rio allowed that was the Tony Morrell he remembered. 'What about him?'

'He has Mexican ancestors, of course. Our cause has fired his blood and he is helping us. He told my father a man named Rio in Los Sequito would help him get safely into the United States.'

'Your father wasn't just after work then – he was running?'

'For his life, *señor!* He had spoken out against *El Presidente* and was betrayed and he had to run. It was all very quick, and the arrangements could not be made properly. There was just no time – I do not understand why he didn't approach you after Antonio telling him you would help.'

'Guess we'll never know why he delayed – but I wouldn't've helped him, anyway, Rosita.'

She snapped her head up at his words.

'I just told you, I can't afford to get mixed up in politics down here. All I want to do is lead a quiet life, make what profit I can, and either make a new life here or head for South America. That's all I'm interested in.'

Her eyes narrowed. 'You are afraid?'

He shrugged. 'Maybe. All I know is that if I get caught up in politics, sooner or later one side or the other is gonna throw me to the wolves back across the Rio. I aim to make it as late as possible.'

'You are selfish – and a coward!' There was heat in her words again now.

'I'm a lot of things – most folk are.' He thrust off the wall and she jerked erect in her chair, very wary. 'Now, you gonna behave yourself for a while and let me get on with my business?'

'And if I say "no"?' Her eyes were watching the small pistol now.

'Then you're a lot more stupid than I think – and I'll lock you up in the root cellar till I'm sure you're gonna be good.'

'You speak like a child!'

'Suits the company.'

'Oh! You are – *irritante! Hijo de puta!*'

He surprised her by smiling. 'As a matter of fact my mother was a whore – she did it because it was the only way she could make enough money to raise me decently. Finer woman I've never met. So you can't insult me that way, *señorita*.'

She slumped, hands falling into her lap. 'All right – you win! I trusted Morelos many times. I think perhaps you tell me the truth. I still blame you for my father's death, but there are others who are to blame, too. I will find out who they are and I will avenge him...' She stopped speaking, looked up at him with those big dark eyes. 'Then you will help me get to the *Estados Unidos*, Rio.'

He made an exasperated gesture. 'For crying out loud, woman, don't you *listen!* I said I won't–'

'I heard you and I understood. But my father had important information, names of people who can help overthrow *El Presidente*. He had to take those names to our friends in your country where they will raise money to help our movement down here. It is nothing that can happen at once, Rio. It will all take time, but we have to get the wheels moving – that is why I must ask you to help me.'

'Save your breath, *señorita*. I'm helping no one but myself.'

Barnaby was just thinking that it was about

time he had some kind of answer to the telegraph he had sent to Zachary Holt in Wyoming when Kelly Treece came into the ranch office.

'Looks like we got visitors, Mister Barnaby.'

'Oh?'

'Comin' down the north-west trail. Dust showin' so I got out the field glasses – I'd say, two-three outriders and what looks like a damn fringed Surrey.'

Barnaby stiffened. 'A Surrey? Out here?'

'Sure looks like it.'

The rancher had a strange feeling that started in his belly and sent a prickly sensation surging through his well-nourished body. He stood up slowly.

'I want you with me, Kelly. Any of the men working around the place today?'

'Crow and Herrick are fixin' the barn roof. Laramie won't be in till later...'

'Tell Crow and Herrick to stand by.'

Treece blinked. 'Stand by...?'

'Yes, dammit, *Stand by!* In other words,

carry on with their work but keep their guns handy and watch out for my signal.'

Treece knew better than to interrogate his boss and nodded, then started out. He turned when Barnaby spoke again, surprised to see the man take a Colt revolver from the desk drawer and begin to check the loads.

'Then come back to the porch and wait until our visitors arrive.'

Treece nodded again and left.

Barnaby sat back in his chair, the gun held in both hands in his lap. *Surely it couldn't be! He wouldn't come all the way down here from Wyoming....?*

Then he felt the wave of sickness wash through him as he remembered just what he had put in that telegraph...

He wished Luis Banda was here.

It was Zachary Holt himself, his fancy gold-headed walking stick in silver clamps alongside his driving seat, soft leather gloves on his hands. His excellently-cut broadcloth suit was dusted from the long trail but he was clean shaven and his hair neatly trimmed where it showed under his wide-brimmed hat. The eyes were surprisingly friendly, but Barnaby felt that was only on the surface.

The two men who rode alongside the handsome Surrey buggy were professionals, Barnaby decided, his heart hammering in his chest, as he watched the smaller of the two, a medium-sized man, swing down easily from saddle.

He walked to the foot of the porch steps where Barnaby stood with Treece. He touched a hand to his hat brim.

'Mornin' – name's Bart Bodine, personal bodyguard and assistant to Mr Zachary Holt, who is the gentleman in the Surrey. You'd be Barnaby?'

'*Mister* Barnaby. What can I do for you?'

Bodine turned his head slightly towards the Surrey. Holt lifted a finger from the top of his gold cane which he was holding in both hands now, and Bodine stepped over beside the vehicle. The other man stayed mounted, hands folded on the saddlehorn, silent and hard-faced. Barnaby thought he looked part Indian.

'Barnaby, I got your telegraph. Now I don't get about too easy these days, thanks to a piece of lead from a bullet put in my hip by a son of a bitch named Brent Rivers. The same man who killed my three sons – which I guess you know about or you wouldn't have sent me a wire and tried to shake me down.'

Holt spoke evenly, almost monotonously, but there was something about the very lack of expression and intonation that knotted up Barnaby's belly. He had to remind himself that this was his ranch, his stamping ground. He called the shots here and it was about damn time he started doing just that.

The way these men rode in it looked like they were taking over. *Time to get things straight.* He cleared his throat. 'I know what I've heard, Holt. I've made you an offer. No need for you to have come all the way down. All you had to do was say "yes" or "no".'

Bodine had looked at Treece and dismissed

him as no real threat. Now he turned cold eyes onto Barnaby. 'Be more respectful, damn you!'

Barnaby made himself swing his gaze to the gunfighter, narrowing his eyes. 'I deal with the top man, not the help – so you stay out of it, Bodine.'

The man's expression didn't change and his gaze didn't waver. Barnaby dismissed him with a curl of his lip and looked back at Holt.

'You tried to shake me down,' Holt said again. 'The bounty I've put on Brent Rivers is $10,000. Your wire says you want double.'

'That's right.' Barnaby felt more confident now: it was about money after all. That he could handle, but he hadn't been sure he could handle a raging, fanatical father with nothing but revenge on his mind. 'My man has located this Rivers and I offered to tell you where for double the price – after all, you've been looking for him for more than two years without success. Now this is a sure thing – must be worth a little more to you.'

'Sure thing, eh? I don't know you from spit, Barnaby. I've heard about you and your high-falutin' ways, insisting on *Mister* Barnaby and so on. That don't make you a big man in my eyes, just one that's unsure of himself and tries to boost his ego and self-esteem by bullyin' folk into doin' what he wants.' Holt spat over the side of the vehicle. 'Got no time for your type. Now if you know where Rivers is, you tell me and I'll pay you $10,000, even though the bounty was literally on Rivers' head. You don't have to go after him and kill him like you should to be eligible for that bounty – so I'm bein' generous, payin' you the bounty for half a job. That's equal to double for the full job. You follow my reasoning?'

Barnaby tried not to swallow but his mouth was desert dry. *So this is why Holt came down himself – saving $10,000 made the journey worthwhile. Now he had to decide whether to push his demands or accept the lesser amount. It was still a mighty big heap of money...*

Barnaby silently cursed himself, knowing he was already weakening, intimidated despite his own back-up, by the presence of Bodine and the Indian, or whatever the other man was.

'I think we can negotiate,' Barnaby said finally.

'That's your answer?' Holt stared until Barnaby nodded and then the crippled man slid his gaze to Bodine and moved his head very slightly.

Treece saw the signal and brought up the rifle he held, but there was a thunder in the ranch yard and he was slammed back against the house wall violently enough for the impact to jar loose one of the oil lamps that hung either side of the door. His rifle exploded into the floor, making Barnaby jump back, and then Kelly Treece crashed face-down on to the porch.

The Indian had moved at the same time as Bodine and his first shot took one of the men on the barn roof in the side. The man staggered, lost his footing, his own gun spilling from his grasp as he yelled and fell off the edge. While he was in mid-air, the Indian put two more shots into him, the body jerking with the impact, seeming to lose all shape when it struck the ground in a puff of dust.

A moment later, the second man's body thudded down only a few feet away. Bodine immediately reloaded his gun, not even looking at Barnaby who was frozen, face greyish-white like the daytime moon hanging above the range.

'Jesus Christ!' he breathed, looking at his three dead ranch hands.

Holt's expression didn't change, nor did the monotonous delivery of his words.

'I believe we have negotiated, Barnaby. What d'you say now to my offer?'

Barnaby was incapable of speech now and merely stared, his mouth hanging partly open. Holt sighed.

'Bart, I believe this fool might need some more encouragement. Start with the barn. We'll work our way up to the house – though

I'd as leave stay there while you go after this Rivers. Oh, yes, Barnaby. You'll tell me where he's hidin', all right. It's a simple deal: $10,000 profit for speakin' a few words or the total loss of your ranch and let's not forget your herds ... and possibly your life. You've got one minute exactly to make your decision.'

CHAPTER 8

KILLERS

Luis Banda noticed the girl at Rio's freight office from where he was watching out of the whorehouse window, and he asked one of the 'soiled doves' if Rio had a woman.

The whore didn't know, said it was unusual for a woman to be seen anywhere near the freighter's except when Monk or old Zutano sent for some company. She was interested in case the girl was a new rival, but Luis made her tell him the layout of the place before sending her on her way with a warning to keep her mouth shut.

'No one must know I am here,' he said coldly and the girl shuddered at the look in his ugly eyes.

He had arrived two days earlier, still

limping from the bullet wound in his leg but able to do away with the crutches now. He used a stick a little but mostly tried to walk without any aid. He had been practising with his gun before he left Texas and was confident now he could beat Rio to the draw.

But as the time drew closer for him to come down and face Rio, that confidence took a couple of dents and he figured out other ways of killing the man instead of bracing him in the town plaza and earning himself a reputation.

It was when he was visiting the whore-house that he noticed the side windows looked out into the freight yard, giving a good view over the high wooden fence, clear to the office and store sheds. So he had made a deal with the *señora* who ran the place to take a room there for a few days. Hell, the bounty would be paid however Rio was killed, so why not a shot between the shoulders or the back of the head...? The man would be just as dead.

And that had been his plan, to bushwhack Rio from the whorehouse window until he had seen the good-looking young *señorita* over there. He still felt a simmering hatred for Rio, the way the man had contemptuously shot him in the leg, as if he wasn't worth wasting good lead on. That did not set well with Banda and he really wanted Rio to know who was killing him, wanted to see the man's face as he put a bullet in him.

The girl seemed to be the answer.

After the young whore had left he brought out his bottle of tequila and a smeared shotglass, poured a couple down his throat and lit a cigarillo, seated back from the window, smoking thoughtfully as he watched the freight yard in the afternoon sun.

Rio wasn't sure just what to do with the girl. He had a notion she didn't want to be seen around Los Sequito – she seemed reluctant to go near the freight yard gate and hung around the men working at their jobs, obviously just filling in time. Rio wanted to get rid of her but didn't know how. He had kept her gun, but she had told him she had a knife and he knew she would somehow lay her hand on a weapon when she made her next try at killing him.

At the same time, he had a hunch that she was not yet ready to kill him. Queer, but that was the impression he had. *She wanted to use him first* – have him smuggle her across the Border into the States, maybe … which meant that she was likely on the run. If her father had been some kind of rebel *politico,* she would be in danger, too, as would any other member of her family. It was *El Presidente's* way: someone defied him and not only that person was killed, but all of his family, too – preferably while the rebel was made to watch. It was a damn brutal regime, all right, but no matter what, he couldn't afford to put a foot wrong.

If he did, he would have to clear out of Mexico and until he could make some sort of arrangements for reaching South America, that meant crossing back into the United

States. A death sentence – thanks to Zachary Holt's huge bounty.

He knew he had been lucky so far that the bounty hunters hadn't tracked him down. That was why he wanted to stay well away from the Border country: he knew it would be watched constantly and he wasn't yet certain that he hadn't been spotted and identified after that run-in with Bignose.

But that was a worry that had been with him ever since he had come down here: he had to live with it. But he had to *do* something about this Rosita de Ayora.

'I have a room over one of the *cantinas*,' he told her. 'Called Cantina Ebano, owned by a man called Jugador...'

'I know this name – it was given to my father. He was told not to trust this gambler.'

'Good advice – but what I'm saying is, there's a bunk behind my office here you can use. If you insist on sticking around.'

She smiled faintly, her eyes slightly hooded. 'I do – I told you, I am going to kill

125

you, gringo. If you do not wish to kill me so you will be safe, then it is on your head, wouldn't you say?'

Rio tightened his wide mouth. 'What I say would make your ears burn. 'I *ought* to kill you, but I don't like killing women in cold blood. I'm not going to try to smuggle you into the US so you can get that out of your head. If it's as important as you say for you to get there and see your friends, or agents, or whoever it is, then you better make other arrangements – see Jugador or the *alcalde*.'

She frowned. '*Sí,* I could do this. And kill you later…'

'Damnit, forget this talk about killing! Go kill Bignose if you want to nail the man who murdered your father, but leave me be to get on with my life!'

This time she laughed, briefly, without humour. Her eyes glinted. 'Ah! You are getting – rattled? Is that the right word, gringo?'

'No! What I'm getting is damn tired of you. Now you can have the bunk behind my office for a couple of nights, then you do something about leaving town. If you don't I'll have you taken somewhere along the trail and turned loose.'

For a moment he saw alarm flare in her eyes and then she curled a lip contemptuously. 'You talk big – I would only come back for you.'

He made an exasperated gesture, yanked down his hat from the peg and jammed it on his head. Snatching up a handful of lading bills he strode angrily to the door, fought the handle as it resisted him briefly and stormed across the yard, calling for Monk, and Zutano.

She was almost laughing as she poked her head out the doorway and called, 'Gracias for the bunk, gringo.'

He did not pause or look around and as she closed the door, she laughed out loud.

But she wasn't laughing a couple of hours later when a dark form slipped into the blackness of the small cubbyhole where the bunk was and reached for her as she reared up in shock, opening her mouth to scream.

A fist crammed the sound back into her throat and her head rapped the wall. Stars burst behind her eyes as she sagged. A rough hand twisted in the thick raven hair and banged her head against the wall once more.

The last sensation she remembered was when the intruder flung her roughly off the narrow bunk and she slammed into the hard floor and passed out.

She did not feel him lift her back on to the bunk, then rearrange her clothing so he could slide his hands against her warm, silk-smooth flesh.

Rio never locked the office door, but he swore when he saw it was standing partly open when he arrived the next morning.

'Damn girl!' he muttered as he went in, tossed his hat at the wall peg, missed, and strode back to the door leading to the bunk room at the rear.

She wasn't there.

All he saw was the mess the bunk was in, crumpled sheets trailing on the floor, the pillow jammed against the wall – with some blood on it. There was little furniture in the small room – an upturned box for a table, a chair with wire-bound legs. Both lay on their sides. He didn't waste any more time, not after he saw more blood on the wall. Not much, but there were a few raven hairs stuck to it and he felt a knotting of his belly as he turned and strode back into the office, instinctively easing his six-gun in its holster.

He stopped dead after two steps.

Luis Banda was standing just inside the outside door, which he had closed quietly. He held a bound and gagged Rosita de Ayora in front of him, her hair dishevelled, a dried streak of blood across one cheek, more blood on the lobe of one ear. Her eyes above the gag were dull, though he felt there was a wildness – or fear – lurking in them. She struggled weakly against her bonds, staring hard at him.

Luis? Well, he had a grin pasted on his face

that stretched from ear to ear.

'*Buenos días,* Señor Rivers! Ah, that surprises you, eh? I know who you are. I know about the bounty – and it will be mine in a few minutes.'

Rio said nothing, still in that frozen attitude, eyes narrowed.

Banda shook the sagging girl a little. 'This is one fine *señorita,* eh? I sample her last night – I think I like her better than the whores next door!' He laughed but Rio's expression did not change. Luis frowned. 'That does not disturb you?'

'Why should it? She means nothing to me – she came here to kill me. I've been wondering what to do about her. *Gracias,* for solving the problem for me.'

That shook Banda. He frowned deeply, seemed as if he wanted to say something but was apparently lost for words. He glanced down at the captive girl, shook her, curled a lip. 'You lie, gringo! You would have killed her.'

'Yeah, I was getting around to that. But

that's a lot of beautiful woman and I guess I was reluctant to turn it into nothing but cold meat.'

Luis smiled slyly. 'So you, too, sample her charms, eh? *Hah!* Then I still have you where I want you! I think I will just shoot you in the belly and then you can watch the *señorita* an' me before I finish you– *Sí*, I like that idea.'

Rio shrugged. 'No need to gut-shoot me, Luis. I don't mind watching.'

Luis's eyes brightened and widened a little, as he ran a tongue across his lips. 'So! The great killer, *the fastest gun alive*, he has the kink, eh? He likes the *miranda furtiva*, eh?'

Rosita's eyes showed shock, too, and then it changed to anger, a killing anger. If she could get free, Rio knew she would try to grab Louis's gun and shoot *him* on the spot. He smiled crookedly.

'There ain't much entertainment in Los Sequito, *señorita* ... I wouldn't figure a gal like you would care...'

She was incensed at his words and struggled violently, straining at her bonds, kicking backwards, ramming her shoulders into Luis Banda. It took the man by surprise and he staggered about six inches away from her.

Rio's gun blasted like a clap of thunder in the small office, twice, and then, as the bullets hurled Luis around and away from the girl, a third time. The man died with a shattered gunarm, a bullet in the chest and a broken spine. The girl staggered from her efforts as the support of Banda's body disappeared and she fell to one knee. Rio reloaded his gun before he stepped forward and pulled her upright. She stumbled against him and immediately fought as well as she could to thrust away from him.

He grinned as he spun her about and took his knife and cut the rawhide binding her hands. She wrenched away so powerfully that she fell across the desk, instantly pushed off and fumbled at the gag with her numbed hands.

Rio stood and watched as Zutano, Monk and two yardmen hammered on the door. He opened it and said quietly:

'Trouble's over. There'll be a body to drop into the tar pit later.'

'Judas!! You – you didn't kill her?' asked Zutano, aghast.

Rio held the door wide by way of answer and they saw Rosita still fighting to drag down the gag and the dead man on the floor. 'Come back later,' Rio said as he closed the door and turned towards the girl.

He was just in time to see her diving for Luis's gun where the man had dropped it. Rio lunged, using his bodyweight to throw her roughly aside. She cried out and fell against the wall, blood-matted hair across her face, gasping. He rammed Banda's gun into his belt, shook a finger at her shaking his head.

'You're a mean little bitch.'

Her eyes blazed. 'You – you insult me! I would kill you for that even if not the other...'

It took him a moment to work that out and then he nodded soberly. 'Well, I had to get you good and mad. I didn't want to shoot through you.'

Her smooth brown forehead puckered in a frown and the fire flickered in her eyes and gradually died as she watched his face. She was silent a long time.

'All right – I believe you. So I suppose I must thank you for saving my life.'

'No need. Saved my own as well. What happened last night?'

She flushed, and, rubbing at her head gently, explained how Banda had attacked her in the bunk room, skimming quickly over the rape. Rio held up his hand.

'Never mind that – I don't have any kink like Luis said. I was just trying to get him confused.'

She started to stand and he reached out to help her, but one look from those dark eyes and he stepped back and allowed her to rise by herself. She rubbed at her wrists.

'He came to kill you for a bounty. He told

me how you murdered the family of a big rancher who will not rest until you are dead.'

'I didn't murder anyone. But I can't go north of the Border because every fool who thinks he can either outdraw me or put a bullet in my back will be after that damn bounty.'

CHAPTER 9

HOLT'S HATE

The girl had two places in her scalp where the skin had split during Luis Banda's assault on her. Neither required suturing so Rio had one of his Mexicans bring some hot water and iodine and clean rags and he sat the girl down at his desk and went to work.

She looked up as he dabbed at the caked blood and mopped up her ear and the streak across her right cheek.

'You are surprisingly gentle – for a gunfighter.'

He said nothing, cleaned the wounds and took a mild pleasure in the way her breath hissed in and her hands clenched when he poured iodine on.

'That more in keeping with your opinion

of me?'

'I know you cannot help the iodine stinging,' she said shortly. 'You are very fast with a gun.'

That didn't require any answer he could think of as appropriate, so he did the final mopping up and dropped the bloody rags into the pink-tinged water.

'I must be loco, taking care of you when you're busting to kill me.'

She dropped her gaze, moved a little uncomfortably in her chair. 'My father must be avenged!'

'Then go after Bignose. He's to blame.'

She curled a lip. 'You like to throw blame on to someone else – I could tell by the way you said you are innocent of murder.'

He stood back, lit a cigarillo, sat down opposite. 'I've never murdered anyone, nor even shot anyone who wasn't trying to shoot me.'

'Of course.'

He sighed. 'Damned if I know why I'm bothering, but you look a mite groggy right now – so while you collect your wits. I'll tell you what happened up in Wyoming.'

'It is of no interest to me.'

'That I believe. And like I say, I don't know why I'm bothering to tell you what really happened but – well, for some reason I'd like you to know.'

She shrugged. 'I would like some tequila.'

He got out a bottle and a couple of glasses, filled them and pushed one across the desk to her. She tossed it down with a jerk, glaring at him, trying to impress him with her toughness. He smiled as he saw the dark eyes filling and her frantic swallowing so she could stifle the cough that tore at her throat. She almost managed it, coughed two or three times into her hand, blinking her eyes as they watered.

He feigned not to notice. Her hand shook as she poured herself another glass. This time she sipped and he kept his face deadpan, leaning his hips against the desk.

He was surprised at how vividly the memories came back. It must be two years now since he rode into Holt's big Flying H spread that fall day and asked for a job...

Two years – and most of that time he had been exiled down here in Mexico, all because of some snot-nosed kid who had never had his butt slapped with a switch or even a bare hand in his life. A spoilt brat – and Holt's youngest son on whom he doted.

Tyler Holt, that was the kid's name. He had two older brothers, Zack Junior, and Kyle. Both were hardworking cowboys and old man Holt sure sweated them. But they had additional duties, too, that kept them mighty busy.

They had to ride herd on Tyler, pull him out of the endless scrapes the kid kept getting himself into. Actually, knowing that his big brothers would fix things, no matter what, had likely gotten him into lots of trouble. He would have figured, what the hell? He had nothing to lose. Zack and Kyle would see him right – or, if it was a real bad one, the Old Man would step in and any problems would literally disappear.

Rio was using his right name at that time, Brent Rivers. Had ridden far from Dakota through bitter cold ice-choked rivers, crossed mountains that came within spitting distance of heaven, and then he came to the Sweet-water Country and the Green River Valley where Holt had his spread.

He hadn't done any cowboying for a long time – it had been easier and more profitable to make a living by the gun: that seemed to be where his talent lay. Zachary Holt had heard of his prowess and hired him on the spot. Rio hadn't wanted to be taken on as a gunfighter, was weary of all the would-bes who braced him wherever he went, testing his gun speed – all dying in their futile attempts to out-draw him.

But he was a long way from his old stamp-ing ground and Holt offered good money, and Rio figured he would be able to talk the man around into letting him have a ranching job sooner or later. Holt had different plans, of course. He was being plagued by rustlers and renegade Indians and even neighbours who didn't care for having their land cut out from under them or shaved way down because of Holt's manoeuvring through legal, though morally suspect, deals he arranged through Wyoming's budding Lands Department. Land he couldn't obtain in this way, he grabbed through sheer bullying and violence.

Up until now, he had used his three sons who had been brought up to take what they wanted – or what their father wanted – at any price. Rio didn't care to be used this way but at the time he was hired, things were quiet enough in the valley and he filled in time practising with his Colt.

Young Tyler watched in fascination.

'Teach me to shoot like that – and draw fast,' he said one warm morning in the still-weak sunlight. He wasn't a bad-looking kid, fair haired, baby-faced, but with a little sadness in his eyes that would bring out the mothering instinct in most women. That was how he wound up with so many and by the time they learned of their mistake there was always trouble at the end.

'It comes natural, kid – a talent. You either have it or you don't.'

Tyler Holt flushed, unused to refusal. 'Maybe I just need a few lessons to get my *talent* started.'

'Maybe that's all it would take – maybe not. You're not going to find out from me.'

The kid glared, even foolishly dropped a hand to gun butt, then paled when he realized what he had done. He was so mad he couldn't speak and stormed off across the yard.

After supper that night, Zachary Holt came on to the porch where Rio was smoking a cigarette before turning in.

'Want you to teach young Tyler how to look after himself. You'll be paid extra. Double what you get now.'

Rio dragged on his cigarette, flicked the butt away so that it landed in a shower of sparks. 'I told Tyler I couldn't teach him anything. He was either born with a talent for gunfighting or he wasn't – I don't believe he was.'

'That don't matter,' Holt said. 'Boy wants to learn a few things about how to handle a gun and as he'll be one of the partners running this spread after I die, I want him to be able to look after himself.'

'You're kinda late.'

Holt bristled. 'The hell d'you mean?'

'Kid gets into trouble, you or your other sons haul him out. He won't ever want it any other way. It suits him fine. But he'll still keep on getting into trouble. Because that suits him, too.'

Holt rammed his glowing cigar against the porch rail, grinding it to pieces. 'You keep your opinions to yourself. You work for me, you do what I say.'

'I don't have to work for you.'

Holt stiffened. His first inclination was to roar and rage and tell Rio to pull his time. But he needed a man like this – needed *this* man. There was a lot of land to the south-west he was interested in. So far his legal men had not been able to find a way of getting it: the owner had it all tightly tied-up with papers and seals and it looked like Holt would miss out. But when Holt had visions of empire-building, nothing was going to stand in his way.

A little softening-up was called for, that was all. It had worked in the past and would work again. Especially if he had a famous gunfighter on his payroll, ready to use his guns on behalf of Flying H...

So Zachary Holt fought down the surge of anger and said more reasonably, 'Rivers, I know the boy has a bad streak in him. I have to use my other sons to look out for him. They don't like it and I won't be around forever to make them do it – so I need to know, for my peace of mind, that Ty can at least take care of himself if he doesn't grow out of this troublemaking habit.'

'He's not going to grow out of it, Mr Holt. It's bred in him and he'll keep doing it as long as there's someone he can fall back on to smooth things over.'

'Well, maybe. But I'll rest easier if I know he can at least use a gun properly. He's had several gunfights, you know.'

'Yeah, I heard.'

'Won them too–'

'Small-town kids, or drunks – they don't count.'

'Look, Rivers, I'm not used to anyone talking to me like this and I've just about reached the end of my patience with you. I'll double what I'm paying you now to teach Ty gunfighting and you'll get another raise when the fighting starts.'

'I'm not hiring on my gun for fighting some dirt-poor rancher who happens to be working land you decide you want.'

'Then it's simple, isn't it?' Holt said between his teeth. 'You don't work for me at all. Draw your time tomorrow!'

Damn! It was said now and he wouldn't – couldn't – back down. Well, looked like he still had that problem in the south-west and though he didn't really want to lose a man like Brent Rivers, it was done now.

'OK – I'll haul out in the morning.'

'Fine. You can have breakfast. No charge.'

Holt wheeled on his heel, a little happier that he had had the last word, and stormed back into the house. Rio sat down on the porch steps and rolled another cigarette.

Just as well, he thought. He was trying to outrun his reputation and working for Zachary Holt wasn't going to help.

He'd move on about mid-morning, head for Montana and the Big Sky Country...

He was strapping his warbag behind the cantle on his horse when Ty Holt came up behind him. Rio turned slowly, saw the kid had had a few drinks. He looked around. The yard was empty. They were rounding up in the high country cutting out mavericks, and Zack Junior and Kyle were leading bunches of men up there. Holt himself was busy down in the river pasture watching his bronc-buster break in an appaloosa he had sent for all the way to the Nez Percé in northern Idaho as a present for Ty's coming seventeenth birthday.

The cook must be busy somewhere, maybe down in the root cellar. So right now there was just the two of them, Rio and Tyler Holt, alone in the big ranch-yard.

'You insulted my pa last night – me, too, from what I hear.'

'Just told him a few truths, kid. Look, simmer down. Don't push this into anything you might regret.'

'*Don't tell me what to do, goddamn you!*' Ty shouted, face reddening. 'I'm sick of people tellin' me what I can and can't do! And you're only hired help!'

'Not even that. Your father gave me a pay slip to draw my time at the bank in town. I'm riding out, Ty.'

'The hell you are!'

Rio shook his head. He could see it happening. Dozens of times in the past he had seen the same thing: some ranny who fancied himself as a gunslinger working himself up till he had enough guts to reach for his Colt.

'Ty, quit this now! I don't want to kill you...'

Ty snorted and Rio knew that was the whiskey making him reckless. 'You *ain't* gonna kill me! I'm faster'n you! I watched you do your fancy shootin'! You might be able to turn a coffee can into shreds but you ain't all that fast.'

'I wasn't trying for speed then, Ty. Don't make that mistake...'

It was too late. Tyler was already drawing and Rio reacted instinctively. His hand blurred down and suddenly there was flame stabbing from it and Tyler Holt was hurled back a few feet, arms flailing loosely, gun spinning out of his grasp, legs folding as he fell.

Rio swore, long and bitterly. It had been pure automatic reaction: he drew against a man pulling a gun on him and without any conscious thought on his part, shot to kill.

He was still bending over the kid's body when the Chinese cook came up out of the root cellar, stooped with his baskets of vegetables, mouth sagging at what he saw.

'You see what happened?' Rio asked.

The cook shook his head. 'No see!'

Rio bit back another curse. Well, this was one gunfight he wished to hell had never happened.

He rode down to the river pasture, not looking forward to this, but knowing he had to try and explain to Zachary Holt. He figured he owed the rancher that much.

Holt was unimpressed. The blood drained out of his face and then he screamed curses, reached for the shotgun on a clip on his saddle beside him, spittle flying. The bronc-buster dived for cover, as did his helpers, and Rio flung himself to one side, drew and fired as a charge of buckshot screamed past his head, some of the balls tearing at his right arm. He rolled on to his belly thumbing back the gun hammer, sweeping the smoking barrel around to cover Holt. But Holt was down, sobbing and writhing in pain, grasping at a bullet-splintered hip, blood splashing. The shotgun was well out of his reach.

Rio mounted, still holding his gun, shirt sleeve bloody, looking down at the wranglers. 'I killed Ty in a square-off – his doing. Holt brought this on himself, too. You saw it.'

'You're dead, Rivers!' Holt's voice was all

distorted with his agony and he was gasping for breath. 'I – I'll hound you to the – ends of the earth! I'll never give up. When I die my sons'll take over. You'll die, Rivers! I'll put such a bounty on your head that even preachers'll start to wonder if they oughtn't go after you so they can build that new church! There's no escape, you murdering son of a bitch! No escape…!'

He didn't even reach the Montana line before Zack Junior and Kyle caught up with him. They found his hidden camp and tried to pick him off from some rocks with rifles. They hit him, twice. Once in the left arm, and again in the calf of his right leg.

Rio knew there was no reasoning with these two: their hatred would be as hot and savage as Old Zack's – and they would be afraid to return without his body. So it had to be a fight to the death.

And it was – Junior's and Kyle Holt's deaths.

They had chosen their time badly. It was

close to sundown. Rio simply held them at bay until it was dark and by then he had bandaged his wounds, stopped the blood flow. He crept around and got behind and above them.

He gave them a chance to throw down their guns but, as he had known they would, they dived away in different directions, trying to disconcert him. It might have worked with a man of normal gunspeed, but Rio was way too fast for their action to matter. *He was already committed.*

He shot them both, one bullet each, dropping them in mid-air.

He sat back in his desk chair, drained his glass of tequila and spread his hands, half-smiling at Rosita.

'And this is how I ended up.'

She was silent, looking thoughtful, then lifted her eyes to stare at him steadily.

'You killed a sixteen-year-old boy. Knowing he could not outdraw you.' There was censure there – or coming.

'He knew it, too – I tried to tell him. He wouldn't listen.'

'So you killed him.'

'I didn't aim for him to use me as target practice.'

'But you *killed* him! You could have only wounded him.'

He shook his head slowly, face sober. 'No. Once I start to draw and I'm facing another man's gun, I shoot to kill – can't help myself.'

'And you killed his brothers – crippled his father.' She threw up her hands. 'You do indeed have *muchas problemas!*'

'Which is why I won't help you. I need to be able to stay here for a spell. Until I make enough to arrange a move to South America – I get caught helping the President's enemies and I'm all through.'

Their gazes locked steadily and then she said very quietly, 'A pity you feel like that – because you are exactly the kind of man I need, Rio.'

CHAPTER 10

TOO MANY ENEMIES

Mister Barnaby felt as if he had come to the end of the trail.

This Holt was like no one he had ever met before. The man was arrogant, crazy with hate and power. He thought there was nothing he couldn't do. And he had this Bart Bodine and the Indian to back him up. Barnaby hadn't heard anyone refer to the Indian by name – only as 'The Indian'. He was a quiet man, had spoken a few gruff words, not enough strung together for Barnaby to be even sure the man could talk enough English to make himself understood.

He seemed to read Holt's mind: Old Zack only had to look at him and the Indian seemed to know just what the rancher wanted. He had shown no emotion what-soever as yet: the killing of the cowhands on the barn roof and Kelly Treece hadn't had the slightest effect on him.

He scared Barnaby almost as much as did Holt himself. And Barnaby wasn't a man who was afraid of much.

Like Holt, he had been used to having his own way, snapping his fingers and maybe a brief order and it was done – or else.

Now he had met more than his match in Zachary Holt. If he hadn't capitulated, told the man where he knew Rio had his freight line, the whole of his ranch would have gone up in smoke and his cattle would have been slaughtered, maybe his men, too, though they came way down Barnaby's list of concerns.

Now he was a virtual prisoner in his own house.

Holt had taken over, kicked him out of his bedroom, commandeered his office, and called in a couple of hardcases from somewhere to keep tabs on the rancher and his men. The crew were puzzled and maybe some of them were a bit leery about these strangers who seemed to be running things but Barnaby, always looking to save face, told them Holt was a prospective buyer and so he was giving the man free run of the place. He knew they didn't believe him but it was some attempt at explanation and he knew the men would obey – for a time, at least.

Holt had sent Bodine to Mexico to seek out this Rio and kill him. He had actually told Bodine to bring him back the gunfighter's head in a gunnysack.

'You're sick, Holt!' Barnaby told him in a brief spontaneous burst of courage.

The bitter rancher had merely looked at him coldly for a long, wintry minute and Barnaby had been surprised to feel the sweat breaking out on his skin.

Barnaby wished he hadn't opened his mouth. He had been going to ask when he would be paid the ten thousand dollars bounty for pinpointing Rio, but common-sense told him Holt would have to see that head in a gunnysack first, so he changed his tack.

'How long before Bodine gets back, d'you think?'

Holt's murderous eyes narrowed. 'There's not a man alive who can outdraw Bart Bodine, no matter what they say about this Rivers. It took me months to track him down – and he's mighty eager to square-off with Brent Rivers. But he won't take any chances. If he doesn't figure he can win in a square-off he'll backshoot Rivers. The man's as good as dead right now, whichever way you look at it.'

Barnaby fell silent. What was there to say? Rio was going to get his and that had to satisfy him.

The girl was bothering Rio more than she ought to. She had changed her attitude to him since he had saved her from Luis Banda. He wasn't sure that she still didn't want to kill him, anyway, but she seemed friendlier and he decided it was because she was trying to soften him up, to win him over to helping her get across the Border.

'Why does it have to be me?' he asked one night after supper. 'Zutano or Monk can likely find someone who'll take you north.'

'I want you to do it.' She hesitated, then said quietly, 'Perhaps it might – even things a little.'

He frowned. 'You mean square me away with you over the death of your father?'

She flushed but her eyes were defiant. 'I may be considering something like that. Then again it might be just my way of making you work harder for me than you did for my father. Then, when we are at the Border, I may shoot you anyway.'

He smiled wryly. 'I don't reckon you'd tell me that if you meant it.'

'Do not underestimate me, gringo! The Ayora are a vengeful family – we never forget.'

'Well, it don't matter, anyway, because I won't be taking you north or in any other direction. You could be on your way tomorrow with someone else. Want me to have a word with Zutano…? I might even stretch a point and send him with you. Then again, if things went wrong I'd be blamed, most likely, simply because he works for me.'

'*Sí*, that is the way of *El Presidente* – but I think you do not know this man very well, Rio. You cannot – ride the fence…?' She paused, looked at him quizzically.

'It's "straddle the fence" or "sit on the fence",' he corrected, mildly amused.

She nodded. 'Well, you must be for *El Presidente* or you are against him – see? You are foolish to think that because you do not help us *revolucionarios* that you will not be persecuted. After all, you are only a gringo and your life means nothing to that monster. He does not like *americanos* because your Government refuses to sell him arms…'

Rio said nothing and she didn't seem satisfied that she had said exactly what she meant.

'Look – I tell you something my father spoke of often. Something he saw with his own eyes and that will show you just how – evil this *presidente* is.' She didn't wait to see if he was interested but plunged on. 'It happened just as he made his coup and took over the post. My father was with some of the loyalists, many of whom had already been shot or tortured by the new *presidente*. He wanted to impress upon everyone that he would have their loyalty – or they would pay a very big price. He had this special regiment, dressed in blue and white uniforms and black, lacquered hats with red plumes. They were said to be made up of the most loyal and most dedicated. To prove it, he ordered a dozen men to fall out, lined them up facing each other, in two rows of six men each. He ordered them to draw their pistols and aim at the head of the man opposite, only a couple of feet distant ... then he smiled at the crowd, and shouted *fuego!*'

She paused and there was a tremor in her voice as she continued. 'They fired – all twelve of those fine young men fell dead. *That* is the kind of loyalty *El Presidente* demands – or obtains by fear and intimidation.' She leaned forward in her chair, face intent. 'Do you see what kind of monster he is now? Men he had personally selected as his Special *Guardia de honor*, treated well, fed at his table, shared his women so it is said. But in the end they meant nothing to him – just so much meat to be used in a demonstration of his power. You wonder why we wish to rebel against such a *diábolo?*'

Rio took out a cigarillo and carefully lit up before answering. 'Yeah, I can see how you're motivated, Rosita. I've heard that story before but I didn't believe it – until now. You made it sound true.'

'It is the truth, Rio! Believe me.'

'I do. And I think this *diáblo* as you call him is overdue for a bullet between the eyes.'

'Then you will help me now?' she asked eagerly.

He shook his head, saw first the surprise and then the blazing fury change her face.

'No, Rosita. I've given my reasons and they still stand. Once I make enough to get to South America, I'm off. I don't aim to get mixed up in any kind of trouble here that'll stop me doing that.'

Her eyes narrowed and he saw her small hands double into fists. 'But we need a man like you!'

'Look around and maybe you'll find one.'

Surprisingly, she said nothing more, merely stood and walked away.

Zutano and Monk had the southern run, only one wagon, but a full load. Then Jugador came to Rio and told him he had a profitable load of tools for a dam development down on the Lagos Gardenas in the foothills of the Madres.

'But we have to pick up the crates at San Bernado, pronto,' the gambler added. 'It will be only a few miles off the usual trail – Monk can drive the spare wagon and they can hire a few local men if they have to so they can load quickly. They will be a little late with the freight to Torreon, but the tools must be delivered first.'

'Hold up. Those merchants at Torreon are

waiting to pick up that load Zutano's carrying. They have to meet the train south and transship it.'

Jugador shrugged. 'That train is never on time – I can arrange for the driver to be "detained" in one of the *cantinas* until Zutano gets there.'

Rio watched him closely. The gambler would never have agreed to that kind of thing before – this must be a *really* profitable run.

'How'd you hear about the tools?' Rio asked quietly.

'I have my contacts. They are unloading at San Bernado because they fear the *bandidos* might try to stop the train and hold the dam engineers to hostage with the tools. The dam is at a critical stage. Some drain cocks have to be fitted and they need these special tools. Rio, I tell you, we pull this off and–' He paused and slapped the heel of a hand against his head. 'Ah! I hate to say it, but you do this and your debt is cleared. *And* you will have profit enough to take a ship to South America.'

Well, it sure was tempting. If Jugador wasn't lying, Rio could make it to safety and by selling the freight line would have enough to start a new business in Bolivia...

But it sounded too good to be true. Yet, when he questioned Jugador until the gambler exploded after repeating the details so many times, he still was a mite uneasy about the deal.

Still, he issued the orders to Monk and Zutano, gave them two extra men and the new Conestoga as well as a slightly smaller one. It meant taking stronger teams, too, for the climb into the foothills, maybe even putting an extra leaf into the wagons' springing. There was a lot of preparation but it went off with a minimum of hassles over the next couple of days, surprising everyone.

The girl had been quiet, staying in the background. He had been too blamed busy to worry about her, anyway. The wagon had cleared Los Sequito a full day and a half when she said to Rio one morning in the biggest store shed:

'I think I must find my own way to the Border – you will have your money soon and you will go to South America.'

'That I will, Rosita,' he said flatly.

'Perhaps it is best. You seem to have too many enemies showing up here, anyway.'

He was busy making final entries to the stocklists and slowly looked up at her words. She was starting to move away, but there had been something in the way she spoke. 'How d'you mean…?'

'Luis Banda came here to kill you – now I hear there is another gringo *pistolero* in town asking questions about you. I think maybe he wishes to kill you, too.'

'Why the hell didn't you tell me?'

'You were busy, very busy. It may be nothing, but I do not like the look of the man.'

'What does he look like?'

'*Malo* – *muy malo*,' she told him quietly. 'His eyes could drill holes in an adobe wall–'

'He got a name?'

'I heard it – Bo? Bo something.'

Rio thought fast. No, he didn't know any gunfighter named Bo – but his could be some bounty hunter who had sniffed him out and–

'It is Bodine!' she said abruptly. 'Sí – his name is "Bodine". You know this man?'

'No,' he said slowly. 'But I heard of a man called Bodine who was making quite a name for himself with a gun up in Dakota before I went to Wyoming. Heard later he killed a man in Deadwood I knew to be pretty good with a gun.'

'He asked for you by the name of "Rivers" – but I think he knows you are using "Rio" because he said he was looking for a man whose real name is "Rivers".'

He looked at her hard. 'You seem to know a helluva lot about what this man has done since arriving in town.'

She looked mildly surprised at his hinted accusation. 'I have been shopping – for my own journey north. He was in some of the places I had to go.' She paused and there was a kind of sly look on her face that she covered very swiftly. 'I think maybe he followed me – here.'

'Just what the hell are you playing at!' Rio flung the lading bills to one side and started towards her, but she backed off, looking innocently surprised.

Then a shadow darkened the doorway of the big freight storeshed and a lean man, looking even thinner against the glare of the sun, lounged against the door frame and tilted back his hat. 'Hell! Is this how the so-called Fastest Gun Alive looks?' He shook his head and spat to one side. 'Man, I 'spected you to be at least ten feet tall and big as a mountain.'

'Who the hell're you?'

'Name's Bart Bodine – and I'm here for a shot at the title, Jack. Then, after I down you, I gotta cut off your head and carry it all the way back to Texas in a gunnysack.'

The girl put a hand to her mouth, making a small alarmed sound, eyes widening. Rio didn't even glance at her. This Bodine was smart enough to stand with the sun at his back, glare distorting him, putting Rio at a disadvantage.

'Where you wanna do it?' Bodine asked. 'Here an' now? I prefer an audience, but ... you call it.'

The man chopped off the last word abruptly and stiffened. Rio could make out movement behind him and then Bodine slowly lifted his hands out from his sides.

'Raise them all the way to your shoulders, *señor*,' said Jugador smoothly. 'You are fast, *señor*, but not fast enough to beat the fall of this shotgun's hammer – unless you would like to bet your life otherwise...?'

'Stop breathin' garlic on me, greaser!' growled Bodine starting to turn his head.

Then he grunted, stumbled into the store shed and fell to his knees, head hanging, hat askew. Jugador covered him with the sawn-off shotgun held in one hand, lifted the man's Colt from its holster and rammed it into his belt. He looked up at Rio and bared his teeth.

'He has been bragging all over town how

he will outdraw you, Rio.'

'Others have tried.'

'Of course – there is a crowd already gathering. This contest has their imagination – two fast guns about to face each other down in our little town's plaza.' Jugador kicked the semi-conscious Bodine to one side and held the shotgun on Rio. Both the freighter and the girl stiffened as the gambler continued to smile and shook his head.

'But, no. The gunfight will be tomorrow – at noon. Not in the plaza, but in the walled *ruedo de toros*. We sell many tickets, Rio, take plenty bets, make a lot of money. We split evenly, me, the *alcalde* and you – providing you walk away, eh?'

He kicked Bodine again and leaned over him. 'You wanna place a bet, *amigo?* I give you odds!'

CHAPTER 11

SHOWDOWN

There was a cellblock in Los Sequito although it was never usually locked. *Usually.* Normally it was kept for drunks and those who needed somewhere to sleep for the night in inclement weather. The fat *policia* expected to make some money off anyone occupying the cells long enough to need food or drink. It was a quiet and profitable little business that helped him keep a young mistress on call.

This night, there were two cells occupied, side by side, only a wall of bars separating them. Rio was in one, Bart Bodine in the other.

It was dark now and they had eaten, each passing over a few pesos to the policeman for some greasy beans and chilli and a cup of strong, excellent coffee. Rio lit a cigarillo and Bodine came to the bars.

'Ain't got a spare have you? Traded my tobacco to that tub of lard for sugar in my coffee.'

Rio stood and handed the man his last cigarillo, lit it for him.

'You freelancing?'

Bodine walked back to his bunk and stretched out, shook his head.

'How'd you find me?' Rio was thinking if his cover was blown he might as well sell off the freightline and move somewhere else. Banda had located him because of Barnaby, but this bounty hunter or whatever he was had seemed confident of finding Rio in this town.

'Looked.'

'Who told you to look?' Rio asked, playing a hunch and Bodine stared hard, blew smoke and said quietly:

'Who do you think?'

'Either Holt or Barnaby.'

'Holt.'

'He never had you on his payroll when I knew him.'

'His family wouldn't be dead if he did.'

'Mebbe. He gonna pay you the bounty?'

'Yeah. You wanna gimme more to ride on out?'

Rio smiled thinly. 'You won't be riding anywhere if that show comes off tomorrow.'

Bodine didn't seem rankled. 'We'll see.'

Rio lay back, shoulders against the adobe wall, smoking and thinking. *This damn circus that Jugador had arranged was going to complicate things. The man simply couldn't pass up a chance at making some money.*

Rio had no illusions: he didn't expect to see any of that money or the bets, despite the gambler's promise to split the take three ways. He knew Jugador too well. And the *alcalde*. The mayor might keep a low profile, but he was always there when the *dinero* was being passed out...

He had sized-up Bodine as well as he could. The man was full of confidence, not quite as brash as he had first appeared when he had shown up in the freight storeshed. That was just him establishing who was boss for the moment. No, the man had a professional look about him, and he had killer's eyes. He moved well, like a cat, smoothly, effortlessly, knowing where he was going. Of course, Rio hadn't seen the man's gun speed, but there were other signs to look for and so far Bodine had measured up in that department.

He was going to be a formidable opponent.

Both men slept well and Rio paid for breakfast for them. Bodine claimed he was broke. It might have been true, didn't matter one way or the other.

Later in the morning, Jugador came to see them, told them the bullring was a sell-out.

'They come in from all over. *Ayii* – if the ring was only bigger! I could delay it all until sundown – or even tomorrow...' he thought aloud, but stopped when he saw the looks on the gunfighters' faces. 'No? You are impatient to see who dies? Very well. Noon today.'

He started to turn away and Rio said, 'Hold up, Jug – I've got things to arrange. Just in case, you know.' Bodine looked surprised at that and smiled. 'I want the freight line to go to Zutano and Monk...'

'Never mind them. They won't be interested,' the gambler said and his words gave Rio pause – there was something in the way Jugador had said that.

Never mind them...

More than just that such men didn't matter, more like – *they won't be here to worry about it.*

Rio's hands tightened around the bars. 'Any word from San Bernado?' he asked quietly, eyes boring into Jugador.

'Not so soon – but won't be long.' The gambler turned to go again.

'Hey! C'mon, Jug! I've got work to do!'

The gambler smiled. 'Perhaps you are already retired and do not know it?' He glanced at Bodine and winked. Bodine gave him a nod that said clearly, *You never know...*

'But – OK. I know you will not run, Rio.'

'You can let me out, too – like to practise before a big showdown,' said Bodine.

Jugador was harder to convince this time and Rio left them to it after the fat policeman unlocked his cell.

He went straight to his freight office and found Rosita de Ayora behind the desk, with some papers. She looked up, surprised to see him.

'I was looking to see if you had some freight to go out this morning. I sent that tallow to the hide merchant yesterday afternoon and the water pump to the *rancho* at El Verde.' She smiled fleetingly. 'I know how important a pump is on a dry farm that depends on wells for its water.'

He was pleasantly surprised and thanked her, but still seemed a little suspicious of her actions.

'Perhaps it is my way of showing my confidence in you to come away the winner today.' She used a bantering tone but he thought maybe she meant it.

He merely nodded. 'Well, I'm free till noon, so I'll get some of the paperwork out of the way...'

He didn't know why it sounded lame, but it did and he saw her slight frown.

'You are – nervous?'

He shook his head, working through some lading bills.

'You are confident, then?'

He glanced up. 'I think Bodine's pretty damn good. It's going to be close.'

Her face straightened. 'Then you must be worried.'

'No.'

'You do not care? Whether you live or die?'

'Of course I do. But I won't know till one second past high noon. No sense in worrying about it till then.'

She watched soberly as he gathered up his papers and pencils and walked across to the storeshed.

They were like a flock of vultures, Rio thought as he opened a new pack of cigarillos and lit up, leaning back in the shade of the canvas awning near the gate used by the *toreros* when this ring was set up for bull-fighting. Somewhere across the sanded and raked arena, Bodine was waiting in a similar shaded entrance, out of sight right now.

The crowd had sweltered all morning in the hot sun, arriving before the large gates of the walled arena were even open. They had packed in with their paper-wrapped *tortillas* and straw-corked bottles of home-made over-sweet *limonada* for mixing with the tequila that the men had smuggled in. There was lots of fruit and he vaguely wondered if he and Bodine would be pelted with it if, for some reason, they didn't put on a show that pleased the paying cus-tomers. But what the hell would be a *lousy* show? If they both missed...? He smiled. Jugador would have some explaining to do then.

The rules were each man had only one bullet in the cylinder of his gun, ready to come up beneath the hammer once it was cocked. The only other rule was the winner had to demonstrate some trick-shooting while the loser was carried out. The crowd had been promised their money's worth.

Jugador was sweating, far more nervous than either Bodine or Rio. He grabbed Rio's arm.

'I have some empty bottles on racks ready to bring into the ring after the gunfight and have set some muchachos collecting old coffee cans. What else can you think of to amuse the crowd afterwards?'

'You confident I'm gonna win, Jug? Or have you asked Bodine the same question?'

One look at the gambler's face and the answer was clear: Jugador covered all angles.

Rio chuckled, shook his head and refused to give the man an answer. Jugador swore, glanced out into the centre of the arena where a post had been driven into the ground. The shadow was very short now.

'Go on out and prepare!' he snapped and Rio was still smiling faintly as he walked out into the glaring sunlight. There were cheers and hisses and boos, depending on which section of the crowd had bet on him or Bodine. The latter appeared on his side of the arena and they walked to the white limewash marks on the ground, about twenty feet apart, slightly to one side of the post. They were on a north-south line and neither would have the glare of the sun in his eyes when the *alcalde* gave the signal to draw. He was to drop a scarlet kerchief from the small dais under an awning where he waited, surrounded by a small group of men and women, important citizens of Los Sequito – and all of whom would have a substantial number of pesos riding on the outcome of the gunfight.

Rio loosened his Colt in his holster, saw Bodine tense, crouch slightly, his hand blurring to his own gun butt. *The man was jumpy!* And that surprised Rio – but he waved a hand briefly indicating that he wasn't anticipating the mayor's signal, just making an adjustment.

But he noticed how Bodine began to

prowl, a few paces this way a few paces back, never taking his eyes from Rio for an instant. He had seen other gunfighters use this tactic, mostly to calm their jumping nerve ends, but sometimes to mask the beginning of the draw during the turn.

He didn't think Bodine was planning on that. The man seemed too intent on being able to claim he had beaten Rio in a square shoot-out, claim clearly and honestly that he was the Fastest Gun Alive. But Rio watched closely, the crowd hushed now as the mayor's arm lifted with the scarlet cloth held between his fingers while he was studying his gold watch ... *Time!*

The kerchief began to flutter to the ground and Bodine dropped to a crouch his gun blazing in his fist.

Damn! Thought Rio even as he felt the bullet strike, staggering him: *he wasn't supposed to draw until the kerchief hit the ground!*

He had fired his own gun even as the flame leapt from Bodine's Colt's muzzle. Now Bodine, starting to stand to get a better look at his handiwork, suddenly stiffened, shuddered, and seemed to leap backwards. Dust rose around his striking body and his arms flew wide so that he landed in the shape of a crucifix, gun skidding away.

'Now you're the Fastest Gun *Dead!*' Rio gritted.

He was crouched over to his left, hand pressed into his side low down, blood oozing between the fingers. He didn't see the crowd surge to its feet, or hear the roar or the curses. But he jumped when a rotten orange squished against his shoulder and he saw grimacing faces amongst the laughing ones, hands raised as they hurled more fruit at him.

The losers, money lost on their bets, sorry he wasn't lying dead in the dust instead of Bodine.

Jugador came running up while other men were assembling a row of shelves to stand the empty bottles and coffee cans on. He thrust a battered box of cartridges at Rio as two men wearing white armbands placed

Bodine on a stretcher and began to carry him out. It, too, was pelted with some fruit and one man even stood on the rails and tried to urinate on the dead gunfighter. The gambler didn't even acknowledge Bodine's death, but he did seem pleased that Rio was the winner. *Counting his pesos,* thought the gunfighter.

'You are not hit too bad,' Jugador snapped. 'Start some trick-shooting or we are going to have a riot!'

Rio looked up, teeth bared, took the box of cartridges in one hand – then smashed the Colt into the middle of Jugador's face with savage force. Blood splashed and teeth and bone crunched as the man collapsed. Rio began to load his six gun with shaking, bloodstained hands.

'You son of a bitch! You fixed me good, didn't you? This damn circus pinpointed me for every lousy bounty hunter both sides of the Border! They'll all know where I am once the word spreads. So I have to make my move, and pronto!'

He pushed the rest of the shells into his pocket, and staggered towards the gate he had come in by. The crowd were still hurling abuse, and the fruit. His side hurt like hell and he could feel the wetness creeping down his trousers.

Now, as it became apparent there was to be no demonstration of trick-shooting, it was all curses, and bottles joined the rain of fruit, making him dodge and stagger.

He turned as he entered the shade and triggered a couple of shots, causing a panic with the people nearby and a pile of struggling bodies. Then he lurched through the short, shadowed tunnel into the sunlight and started to turn towards the small creek where he had stashed the palomino with full saddlebags and rifle in the scabbard.

As he had told Jugador, he was forced into running now, before everyone and his goddamn brother tried to collect that ten-thousand-dollar bounty... *Curse Zachary Holt!*

The world was swaying and going in and

out of focus. His mouth was hot dry as a dust storm, the pain in his side spreading through his body. He stumbled to his knees, stayed there, one hand down on the ground wondering if he would have the strength to rise again.

Then he groaned as he heard horses racing towards him.

Hell! It was too late!

He fell forward on his face in the dust.

CHAPTER 12

TO THE BORDER

There was a coldness and a dank smell. Maybe a hint of dust. He shivered.

These were the sensations he awoke to, slowly, painfully, his eyelids feeling glued together so that it required effort to open them. And then it was as if he was trying to see through a fringe of branches or torn sacking. There was dimness all around him: not quite full darkness, but close. It was something he felt rather than saw at first.

After a while it began to turn grey and then a lighter grey still, but no better than that. But he could see – and he was staring up at an overcast sky with slowly scudding clouds, the window of his sightline edged in ragged straw. He blinked, thought about

184

that, turned his head and felt the stiff muscles in his neck and shoulders.

He was lying on some blankets which were spread on a layer of leaves or straw and he saw scabbed adobe walls, one crumbling, and he thought, 'Wherever this is, it seems to be abandoned and falling to pieces.'

He was right on both counts and then he saw the girl, and someone not quite within the ambit of his vision, back in the shadows. Rio thought he spoke but all he did was make a grunting noise. It was enough to bring the girl's head around sharply from whatever small chore she was attending to.

Then she was kneeling at his side, looking anxious. 'You are feeling better?'

'Dunno how I felt before, but this don't feel what I'd call – "better". Better'n being dead, I guess.'

His mouth twitched and she realized he was trying to smile. She arranged the blankets, lifted the edge halfway down his body, nodded.

'Bueno! The bleeding has stopped. You

may have a cracked rib or two, but there doesn't seem to be any other damage.'

He frowned, working at sorting out her words and trying to relate them to what she had said. He began to remember then – the staged gunfight, Bodine trying to beat the signal, the bullet tearing into his side, running the gauntlet of the suddenly hostile crowd and then falling, with the sound of horses coming towards him...

His gaze sharpened. 'You brought horses?'

'I followed you when you left your palomino down by the creek with full saddle-bags and other signs of you getting ready to clear out. I, too, prepared a mount and after the gunfight I went straight to the creek to wait for you – I knew you would have to go, too. Once word got out about the gunfight you would have bounty hunters dogging you day and night. When I saw you fall, I rode out, managed to get you into the saddle and came here.'

'Which is where?'

'An old abandoned adobe inn set off the

trail back amongst thick timber. It looks very old.'

'I can see by the walls.' He was straining to see who the other person in the dim room was but could only make out that it was a man. He tensed. 'I wouldn't've figured you'd know about this place, though.'

She saw the direction of his gaze and smiled slowly, pointing to the shadowed figure. 'This man told me about it. Yesterday.'

The man came forward and Rio stared hard as he recognized the *alcalde*. 'The hell're you doing here?'

The mayor gave a shrug and a kind of tight-lipped grin. 'I thought you would make your run after the gunfight, *amigo*. It was really all you could do. And Jugador, although he has been my – no not *compadre* – but my *asociado* for a long time, more and more he had been – what do you say? Something about "crosses"?'

'Double-crossing you.'

'*Si!* Double-crossing me on many small deals. Little things, maybe, but starting to grow. This time I knew he would not be able to resist some kind of trick with so much money at stake – and I was right. Before the crowds had settled in he arranged for the money to be taken to the bank – and deposited in his name only.'

Rio was tired and slow to understand but he nodded slightly. 'Sounds like Jug. Means I'm out, too, but I expected it. That's why I decided ahead of time to quit.'

The mayor smiled widely now. 'Jugador will never forget you – or forgive you! You have ruined his face for all time and you know how he felt about women...'

Rio said nothing to that but he did feel kind of good. He had owed that damn gambler more than money for too long a time. He looked from the mayor to the girl.

'How'd you two get together?'

The *alcalde* gave that characteristic shrug and innocent look again. 'I have – er – helped the people the *señorita* is involved with from time to time.'

'So they weren't all wetbacks – even before

I suspected some were *politicos* on the dodge.'

'The *alcalde* – and your friend Jugador – arranged for arms to be sent to our people and helped our fugitives get away.' She paused, looked at the mayor's amused face and then back to Rio. 'Not all the freight you carried was innocent, I'm afraid Rio.'

He closed his eyes and it seemed a long time before he opened them again. 'You son of a bitch,' he told the mayor but without much heat. 'Serves me right for not being more on the ball. I guess I was more interested in looking out for my own skin, watching for bounty hunters and so on. I'm lucky I lasted so long in the freight business.'

'Oh, but you were useful, Rio, *amigo*, now you are going so it is time for me to look after myself.'

'Oh? You hadn't been doing that all along?'

The mayor laughed. 'OK! OK! But this time Jugador has fleeced me once too often. He is finished here, he knows that – but he has one final move against you, Rio. Even through the pain of his face, he sent a man to take a message to *El Presidente's* agents to the south. I am sorry, but your two friends, Zutano and Monk – they will be imprisoned by now, if they haven't already been shot.'

The girl put a hand on his shoulder as Rio struggled to rise, staring hard and coldly at the mayor.

'And why should that be?'

'Come, Rio! You did not suspect anything about these boxes of "special tools" that had to be shipped so pronto to the engineers at the Lagos Gardenas dam?'

'Yeah – I suspected something, but I thought if they were guns for the rebels then Jugador would have fixed everything at the other end.'

'*Si*, but since then, you have ruined his face, Rio. I told you he would not forgive. He would rather lose the money from the sale of those guns just to put you on the run as a *contrabandista* – and that is what will happen as soon as the *rurales* stop your wagons and open those cases marked tools. You are a

190

fugitivo, marked for death now.'

Rio slumped. There was concern on the girl's face. The mayor said he must return to Los Sequito before dark and prepared to leave.

'*Adios*, Rio. I think we will not meet again.'

'I'm not gonna say it's been nice knowing you, *alcalde*, but it hasn't been all that bad.'

The mayor smiled and left and they heard his horse going away from the ruins.

'I am sorry, Rio,' Rosita said. 'You are involved in politics now whether you like it or not. And I am sorry about your friends, but there is nothing you can do.'

Rio knew that. For one wild moment he had thought he would wait until he was fit enough and then ride south and break out Zutano and Monk from whatever prison they were in. But as the mayor had said, it was likely they were already dead – the *rurales* had a habit of shooting gun-runners on the spot.

He was penniless and wounded – and on the dodge. Not just from bounty hunters and assassins, but from *El Presidente's* personal wrath now.

South America looked mighty good – but such a damn long way away. With no chance of getting any closer.

Two days later, Rio couldn't wait any longer.

His wound was sore but healing – or beginning to. The girl warned him he should rest for another few days.

'You risk it opening again if you move around too soon.'

'Tighten the bandages,' he told her shortly. 'We can't stay here. Sooner or later someone's gonna come, even if it's only a courting couple stumbling in looking for a bit of privacy.'

'You *must* wait, Rio! Where can you go?'

'I've got it figured.' His face was gaunt and grey, but he was sitting up now and had been walking around the ruins slowly, using the low, crumbling walls for support when he needed it. 'Rosita, I owe you plenty for all you've done, not just here, but previously.'

'Do not mistake my motives for compassion, Rio,' she said quietly.

'I know – you still need to avenge your father and you still want to make contact with your friends across the Border. OK – I've got to get out of Mexico. I'll take you to where you can cross into the States and then I'll head on down to Vera Cruz or one of the other Gulf ports where I can pick up a ship to South America.'

Her face was sober, studying him. 'I have used you, Rio – manipulated you. I must be honest with you.'

He smiled crookedly. 'I'm dumb but not that dumb I can't figure things out for myself. Anyway, I think I knew all along that sooner or later I was going to take you to the Border.'

Her face softened. '*Gracias,* Rio! I could have made other arrangements, I suppose, but – somehow – I wanted it to be you.' Then she frowned. 'But we will need money! I have a little, but very little. You?'

'Not even the price of a pack of cigarillos.'

'Why do you sound so cheerful about it?'

'I'm not, really – but I know where to get all the money we need.'

'How? Where?'

'Where is a lot of money usually kept, Rosita?'

'Well, obviously a bank – but you don't mean that. So where d'you–' She gasped suddenly. *'Aiiyeee!* You *do* mean a bank! You are loco, Rio! Loco!'

'Aw I dunno. I reckon the Los Sequito bank will give me what *dinero* I need. And if most of it happens to belong to Jugador – well, he's a gambler. This is just one hand he's going to lose.'

She shook her head slowly. 'I like your idea of stealing from Jugador – but Rio, you will never be able to get away with it! There are armed guards in that Bank – they will shoot you down.'

'Not if I use the right kind of shield.'

He sounded so confident she felt lost for words.

Just as the bank was closing its doors for

siesta, when all the businesses closed for a couple of hours during the afternoon, Rosita de Ayora came bustling along the boardwalk and smiled at the armed guard as he shot home the floor bolt on one door. She started to sidle past him into the bank's dim interior but he stood, blocking her way.

'Time for siesta, *señorita*,' he told her heavily using his bulk to edge her back.

But she resisted and he frowned, big and hard-looking, a hand hovering near his belt pistol in its flap holster.

'I have urgent papers for the *alcalde*,' she said, showing the man a sheaf of papers in her handbag. 'He told me they must be deposited in the bank's vaults immediately.'

The guard was puzzled but hesitated. He had seen this woman with the mayor once or twice lately. It was more than possible she was the *alcalde's* latest mistress. He glanced around. Some of the clerks were already gone, others were still at their counters behind the grilles. Two customers were completing their business.

'Take me to the *jefe!*' snapped Rosita impatiently. 'And I will have something to say to him about your obstructing the *alcalde's* business!'

The guard made a placating sign with his hands, stood aside. 'It is still a few minutes to the precise siesta time, *señorita*,' he said, sweating heavily now as he forced a grin. 'I did not realize…'

She was already inside and hurrying towards the nearest counter still manned by a clerk. The man gave a heavy sigh when he saw her taking papers from her bag. A deposit for the vault, he concluded, correctly, which meant writing out deposit slips, receipts which had to be counter-signed by the *jefe* himself – and the man thought the bank manager might already have slipped away. He had a young and beautiful wife waiting in a cool house on the only hill near town.

As Rosita began explaining she was acting for the mayor and that the papers had to be put in a sealed envelope, she saw the other

196

two customers who had just completed their business starting towards the door where the guard waited to usher them out, holding the door half-open.

Then suddenly the door was smashed back into the guard and he staggered and a man burst in holding a sawn-off shotgun, a bandanna masking the lower half of his face.

'*Hola, hombres!*' He swung towards the guard who was staggering upright, reaching for his gun. The shotgun's barrels slammed against the man's head and he dropped. The masked man spun back as the second guard moved forward, gun in hand. The shotgun lifted, both hammers cocked. The bandit spoke in Spanish. 'If you would live, *señor*, you will stop now and drop your *pistola!*'

The guard wanted to live – he was a married man. His gun thudded to the floor. The bandit made him kick it under a counter and with hands raised, he faced the wall, sweating.

The bandit covered the two clerks still on duty and they lifted their hands.

'All the money from the shelves – those there.' He pointed to the big vault which stood behind the clerks, doors open, stacked with canvas bags and piles of currency and coin. 'The bags marked Cantina Ebano first – then whatever else you can cram into this sack.'

He tossed a gunnysack he had pushed into his belt towards the clerk and gestured impatiently to Rosita as it caught up in the bars of the grille. 'Push it through, *por favor, señorita. Ah, gracias!*'

Rosita looked pale and frightened as she obeyed and the clerks hurriedly began to transfer the money bags into the gunnysack. The bandit kept looking around. The door was now closed behind him. The streets were emptying as folk headed home for their siesta hour. The guard on the floor groaned and dazedly rubbed at his head. The one against the wall began to tremble.

'*Prisa! Prisa!* Hurry it up, you *burros!*'

The frightened men hurried up and then the bandit ordered the nearest one to push the bulging bag over the top of the grille. He did so and it flopped heavily to the floor near Rosita. The bandit stretched out his left hand, the shotgun still menacing in his right, and snapped his fingers.

'If you will, *señorita!* Pronto!'

Visibly shaking, Rosita picked up the sack of money, not taking her eyes off the wild-eyed bandit, held it out towards him, but she was still several feet away. He snapped his fingers and growled impatiently and she stepped across, thrusting the sack at him.

'You keep hold of it – and if you let it go, I will kill you!' he warned her, still in Spanish, and she cried out as his arm went about her waist and he pulled her tightly against him, shielding his body.

'No! No!' she screamed and struggled, but stopped when the muzzles of the shotgun pressed up under her chin. Her eyes bulged and her legs seemed unable to fully support her.

The bandit began backing away towards the door, dragging her with him.

'Remember – you drop the sack and you die, *señorita!*'

'Help me, please!' Rosita screamed and the guard standing against the wall, swallowed, didn't look around, closing his eyes.

Then one of the clerks brought up a gun from under the counter and the one who had been serving Rosita screamed:

'Don't shoot! She is the *alcalde's* woman!'

The clerk with the gun widened his eyes but fired a shot anyway, too nervous to control his movements. The bullet spanged off the brass bars and ricocheted from the steel door of the safe, causing the alarmed clerk to yell as he dropped to the floor, throwing the gun from him.

The bandit was at the door now with his hostage and told Rosita to turn the handle. Then the guard on the floor suddenly came to life, rolling fast, bringing out a gun that had been hidden by his prone body and she heard the robber curse – in American.

'Goddammittohell!'

The guard's gun came up and it was clear

he would shoot no matter what. The shotgun thundered, drowning the shot from the pistol, and the guard screamed as the buckshot took him in the lower legs, kicking the limbs out from his body and slewing him around. He began to whimper, clutching at his mangled leg.

Then the robber and the girl were outside and on the almost deserted street, only a few startled townsfolk stopping to stare as the man dragged the girl around the corner into a narrow alley and ran down it towards where, no doubt, a getaway mount was waiting.

Only long afterwards did one witness, a swamper at the Cantina Ebano, remember that it seemed as if the girl hostage was actually running of her own free will down the alley, clutching the gunnysack of money tightly to her.

He thought, too, that he had heard a woman's bright laughter coming from the alley, just before the clatter of hoofs.

CHAPTER 13

RIO'S RUN

'*Tonto! Idiota! Hijo da puta!*' Jugador's screaming was too much for his wounds and they burst, blood spreading in widening red splotches under the bandages that swathed his head. He sobbed a curse and put both hands to his face, holding gently, rocking back and forth in his bed.

The men, including the *alcalde*, who stood around in the room moved uncomfortably. Except the doctor. He muttered something and lunged for the bed, easing the raging gambler back on the pillows.

'Señor! You must stay calm! *Aiiiyyyeee!* You have done much damage already! The *sutura* have split .. I will have to do it all over again!'

'Get away from me, you butcher!' There was real pain in Jugador's voice, only his swollen eyes showing now. They were deep-set in bruised flesh but they glinted. He raked his gaze around the others. 'It was *him! It was Rio!* Don't you see that? He and the girl – they arranged it between them ... she wasn't a hostage! She *helped* him! All my money! Aaaaah!'

'In the name of *dios, señor!*' pleaded the doctor. 'Look at the blood.'

He fussed around, Jugador pushing him aside, but the medico coming back determinedly. The gambler looked past the weaving head and hands.

'They say she was depositing papers in your name!' he accused the mayor who looked surprised – and innocent.

'I know nothing about it! If, as you say, she and Rio arranged it all between them, then they also arranged for her to say that – so she would seem a more important hostage, no doubt, someone connected with me. You forget, Jugador, that one half of that money was mine, too.'

Jugador hadn't forgotten. He hadn't even thought about it because he had deposited all the money from the gunfight show in his name only. The mayor knew this – but was just reminding him. Not that it would do him any good.

'You have men searching, of course?' he asked lamely.

'Of course. We will find them and bring them back. With the money – which we will share, also, "of course".'

The mayor's eyes were hard as he looked at the gambler trying to mask the terrible pain he felt. The doctor said he would never be the same. His face would be scarred and misshapen. Women would shy away from him. Men would avert their eyes…

'It was almost worth it,' the *alcalde* thought ruefully. Almost – losing his share of the money just to see Jugador at last beaten down. Perhaps now, *he* would be able to run this town his way, instead of just being a figurehead for this greedy madman.

Oh, the mayor had prospered in his relationship with Jugador over the years but now – well, he hated to admit it even to himself, but there was a little more silver in his hair, a little less steel – where it counted more... He was ready for a quieter life, with less risk attached. But the lift to his spirits to see Jugador in such a position as now! Aaaah! It was most – agreeable.

Yes! he decided. It definitely would be worth it.

If they recaptured Rio and brought him back with the money – well that would be a bonus.

But for now he felt a deep satisfaction with the way things had gone.

He was top man for now – and intended to stay that way.

The wound in Rio's side was giving him some trouble, but not so much that he couldn't hide it from the girl.

The escape from Los Sequito was easy enough. They had taken a couple of horses from the corrals behind the big town stables where the workers were already enjoying their siesta, then stashed them at the end of the alley beside the bank. They rode through the back blocks of the town to where they had left their own mounts, all saddled and supplied and ready to travel, Rio's palomino, the girl's sorrel.

Things were only just beginning to stir back in the town by then – all the rubber-necks and citizens who had been disturbed by the shooting standing around and discussing it as was usual with the Mexicans of Los Sequito, making up their minds what to do and who was to do it.

By then they were into the foothills and losing their trail amongst the stony draws and gulches, working the horses hard throughout the afternoon. By sundown they were far from the town and had laid a false trail leading due north.

Actually they were heading north-east – if they had been on a ship the heading would have been stated as *nor' – nor' – east.*

Over the two years he had been down south of the Border, and using his early days with his growing freight line as a cover, Rio had searched out many hidden places and secret trails. A man with ten thousand dollars riding on his head needed to have more than one bolthole. So far he had been lucky, but whatever luck he had had was beginning to run thin. Fair enough – he had had a good run and it would have been even better if he hadn't fallen under the power of Jugador. He had allowed it to happen simply because he didn't want to make any kind of fuss that would draw attention to the remote place he had chosen.

Well, that was over now and he even had some of the money he had hoped to get together. Of course, the freightline was gone – its value would have enabled him to set up right away in South America. As it was, he would have enough to go south to Bolivia and maybe establish some kind of business there. It would be small and take time before he could relax, but it would be a long way from Zachary Holt – and that vindictive son of a bitch, Barnaby.

He even had some pleasant female company – for now. He wasn't sure about Rosita de Ayora. More and more she was showing signs of what he thought of as growing fanaticism – at first he had termed it 'mild' fanaticism, but then he figured that was like saying someone was only a little bit pregnant. It didn't work – you were or you weren't, no midway.

She had led him to believe she was only on the fringe of this burgeoning revolution at first, more or less pushed into it simply because she was her father's daughter. But she seemed familiar with this Estrada and there were signs she was part of an established network. And now, forced to run, she knew where she was going. *Pre-arranged probably* – and using him to get her there. He had no illusions. She wasn't interested in him as a man – although she hinted strongly enough that this was not necessarily something that she would dislike – but rather she was more interested in what he could do for her fellow *revolucionarios.*

She wanted him on-side so he would use his astonishing gun speed to help her and her friends.

Well, that wasn't on Rio's agenda. Bolivia was. He would see the girl safe before he rode for Vera Cruz or some other Gulf port, but that would be it.

The first night camp was one without fire and they ate cold chicken which she had brought from town, with day-old bread. He spooned up a can of beans as well and they washed it all down with canteen water.

'Do you know where there are streams clean enough to drink from?' she asked him.

'I can find some, I reck-on.' A stab of pain caught him and made his breath catch, adding an extra syllable to the word. She glanced at him sharply. 'Your wound – it troubles you?'

'It's OK, – I've drunk water from a three-day-old hoofprint when I had to and once I ate a cat.' He was trying to divert her from the state of his wound and this last likely did it.

She was starting to get up to come and examine his wound but stopped in mid-action. 'A cat? You mean–?'

'Yeah, a common domestic cat. Up in Nebraska. I was on the run and broke, hunting for whatever food I could get, mid-summer in dry country, hotter'n the hinges of Hades. I tracked down a brush turkey and she led me all over the countryside. I didn't want to shoot at the time and maybe draw the posse. I figured the turkey was giving me the runaround because she had chicks somewhere and was trying to lead me away from 'em. Anyway, I found the nest and there was only the one chick, few weeks old, plump because momma had been bringing it plenty of food. I grabbed it, wrung its neck and cooked it over my fire. I ate half and stashed the rest in a sack high up in a tree.'

'You had a camp then?'

'Sort of. To cut the story short, I came

back from staking out my horse on a patch of grass, just in time to see this big orange cat I'd noticed on a ranch not too far from where I was camped, licking its chops over the bones of my half-turkey chick. I was good and mad – I'd been hounded for two weeks, didn't have two cents to rub together and was faced with a mountain crossing that once I started I didn't dare stop. There would be no time for hunting food. That half-turkey would have seen me across ... now I had no grub at all.'

She was wrinkling her nose by now. 'You – killed the cat? But it must've been hungry, too!'

'Like I said, I was good and mad. I picked up a rock and threw it at him hard. Caught him in the head and he dropped where he stood purring at me. I was going to throw him away when I felt all that pampered flesh under his fur and thought hell, he can see me over the mountain ... and he did.'

She stared at him, trying to make up her mind whether to believe him or not. 'Wh-

what did you do?'

'I skinned him, stopped long enough to singe the flesh in a fire and ate him in the saddle.'

Her distaste was showing more and more. 'And what did it – taste like?'

'You know that kinda pee smell cats have…? Like they leave behind in a room or wherever they've been? That's how it tasted. But it got me over the mountain and safely away from the posse – always had a soft spot for cats since then.'

She watched his face but he merely snapped a match into flame on his thumbnail, swiftly hiding the flare in his cupped hands, and lit a cigarillo. He hid the glowing end in the curve of his right hand, exhaling smoke as he watched her.

'Guess you're not used to living rough.'

She hesitated and then said, 'I think I am learning. When I had to run after my father tried to get across the Border, I had to stay with some of Estrada's rebels in the hills for a day or so. How many days – and nights –

to the Border now?'

'Well, we got to take trails where they won't look for us. Adds a lot of time and a lot of miles. But we ought to make it in three, four days.'

'Where will we cross?'

'That again depends on how close they are behind us – and, it won't be "we". It'll be just you.'

She sobered. 'But, Rio! There is nothing for you down here now! You could help me and my friends and you would be rewarded.'

He shook his head, slapped the bulging saddlebags that contained the money they had stolen from the bank. He hadn't bothered to count it yet.

'I'll have enough to get to Bolivia and set up some kind of business. I'll get you to where you can cross safely, but I'm not setting one foot in the United States. After I see you right, I'm heading south – wa-ay south.'

He made it sound final and she made no reply. But she looked sad – and dis-appointed.

The next day they sighted a dust cloud in the southwest, coming from the direction of Los Sequito. He lay for a long time on a boulder just below the crest of a ridge, studying the cloud through battered field glasses. She heard him swear.

'What is it?'

'I see the flash of metal and maybe leather – I'd say that's a troop of *rurales*. And there are other riders, too. Civilians, I guess. They must have a good tracker.'

She showed alarm. 'What can we do?'

'Lay a trail up and over this ridge – there's really no other way to go.'

'Then why leave a trail to show where we crossed?'

'Because I aim to take us across the top of that cliff and drop down between this ridge and the next and lose whoever it is.'

Rosita went pale, looking up. 'But there is no trail up there! There is not enough room!'

'No – we'll have to *make* room, after laying the false trail over. Gonna be pretty dangerous but it's the only way I can see out of this.'

She stared, lips parted slightly and he heard her breath coming hard. 'The – only – way...'

'Well, we could stop and make a stand – not really an option.'

She swallowed audibly. 'Then we have to take the cliff trail ... I – I do not like heights!'

He admired her for that, seeing how much it cost her to agree to his wild plan.

Later, when they started along the crumbling edge of the vertical cliff, lost against the grey-green of the vegetation, a dizzying drop on their right to sun-cracked rocks three hundred feet below, she called and in a small voice, said:

'I trust you, Rio!'

He made no reply, but he wondered what she would say if she knew that by taking this trail in order to avoid the *rurales,* having no real choice in the matter, they would be heading into territory claimed by the *bandido* who was called Bignose.

CHAPTER 14

JUST – ADIOS!

Barnaby was starting to get dressed in the small bedroom he was now using in his own ranch house when he heard the thud outside in the hall.

He was going to ignore it, but there were growling sounds like someone trying to talk – or in pain. He had just been looking out of the window and had seen the stoic Indian getting Holt's buggy ready down by the barn. Holt must be going on another tour of inspection of the big ranch. Son of a bitch was talking about 'buying-in' – whether Barnaby liked it or not…

Thinking about how he was being treated – and afraid to do anything about it, which made things worse – Barnaby strode to the door, half-dressed, and looked out into the hallway. He smiled crookedly.

Holt had fallen, right at the top of the stairs leading to the living part of the ranch below. The man was groping for his gold-headed walking cane, hair tousled, eyes reddened and watery from his bout with the bottle last night. Word had come in that Rio had outgunned Bodine in some sort of circus in the local bullfighting ring at Los Sequito. He had been upset that Bodine hadn't managed to kill Rio – not at the gunfighter's death – and had complained bitterly that if it was true and it had all taken place in public, then Rio would be on the run again – and it might take him years more before he tracked the man down.

He called for whiskey and had gotten through two bottles before Barnaby had gone to bed. The hard-eyed rancher had become maudlin over the loss of his sons, weeping openly, something Barnaby had thought he nor anyone else would ever witness in Zachary Holt. But the man was in his cups well and truly and had had an arm about the shoulders of the impassive, non-drinking Indian, slurring his words as he told the story of his loss over and over.

Barnaby had heard the Indian dragging Holt to his bed sometime in the early hours. Now the man had woken, no doubt hung-over or even still half-drunk, tried to get downstairs for a bracer – and fallen instead.

Now he set his bleary eyes on Barnaby as the man walked slowly along the hall to where he lay. Holt reached up with a trembling hand.

'Help me up!'

Barnaby merely stared down, his heart racing. The Indian was outside, hadn't heard anything. His own staff were in the big kitchen attached to the back of the house. There was just Holt and himself here, just the two of them...

'Say "Please *Mister* Barnaby",' the rancher said.

Holt blinked, 'What?'

'You heard, you son of a bitch! Call me

Mister Barnaby!'

Holt was only keeping himself from falling by one hand gripping a rail. He was lying on his bad hip and it was obvious by his face that he was in a great deal of pain. He glared up at the rancher, tight-lipped. Only when Barnaby made to move back to his room, did he say, haltingly, quickly: 'Please! *Mister* Barnaby! Help me – please! I'm falling.'

Barnaby seemed to consider it and then as Holt started to curse, strolled back and grabbed the man beneath the arms and hauled him upright. Holt cried out in pain.

'Careful! You goddamned fool!'

'Yeah, I have been just that – but no more. I'm all through with you, Holt. And you're all through – period!'

Standing the man on the top step he suddenly hurled him as hard as he could down the stairs. Holt cried out, but as his head smashed through some side rails and his body tumbled and flailed and somersaulted all the way down, his cries were stilled. He crashed on to his face and

Barnaby, who had been following quickly, reached down, grabbed the man's head and wrenched it back, snapping the neck. Then he ran back up, throwing the gold-headed cane down the stairs, and hurried into his room, breathing hard as he heard the Indian running into the house.

He gathered himself, tousled his hair, ripped open his shirt and undid the belt of his trousers, stumbling out into the hall and to the top of the stairs. He was still holding up his trousers, looking like a man who had just jumped out of bed, awoken from a sleep by something that had shocked him, and was now coming to investigate.

He paused at the top of the stairs, looking down on the Indian's back as the man knelt beside Holt.

'Godalmighty! Is that what the racket was ... he all right?'

The Indian looked up, flat face unreadable. 'Dead. Neck broke.'

'Judas! Christ ... must've had one helluva hangover! And no wonder after all that red-eye he put away.'

The Indian stood, looking up at Barnaby.

The rancher felt uncomfortable. 'What now?'

After awhile the Indian shrugged. 'No job now – I go.'

'Well, maybe I could use a man of your talents…'

The Indian shook his head. 'Can't work for you.'

'Why? My money's as good as Holt's.'

'Can't work for dead man.'

Barnaby blinked, it sinking in suddenly, and his mouth sagged and he started to turn to run but the Indian's gun roared and the rancher lurched with the strike of lead. He teetered for a moment and then tumbled down the stairs to sprawl at the Indian's feet.

'Holt say somethin' happen to him, kill Barnaby.'

Eyes glazing, blood trickling from his mouth and his chest smashed in by the bullet, Barnaby's last words were:

The girl had been pretty quiet since the traverse of the cliff top. It had been nerve-wracking, the edge crumbling under the frightened horses' feet, but the animals'd had enough sense not to toss or buck, knowing that to do so would mean they would all fall off the cliff.

To make the girl feel more secure, Rio had passed a rope from his saddlehorn back to her and she had tied this around her slim waist, holding to it with one hand while he negotiated the narrow, dangerous path. The palomino was actually make it as they progressed, thrusting dry, stabbing brush aside, sending cascades of gravel and crumbling rock spilling out into space.

It had taken so long that Rio was afraid the *rurales* and the other pursuers might easily see them while following the false trail he had laid up the slope and over the crest of the ridge, a mile away. But somehow they had made it and the girl refused to let him undo the rope until they had ridden down into the big draw between the hills.

At the bottom, they each drank deeply from their canteens. He watched her and when their gazes finally locked, she thrust out her jaw and tossed her head.

'Well?'

'We should keep moving.'

'Then lead the way,' she told him shortly. 'You say you know this country ... I'm in your hands.'

He said nothing, coiled the rope, hung it over the saddlehorn and started his horse forward again. She rode after him, closing the gap as they entered deep, cool shadow, looking around, one small hand on her saddle gun.

'This feels dangerous country.'

He rode on a spell before answering. 'Getting into *bandido* territory now – all the way from here to the Border.'

She snapped her head up. '*All* the way?'

He nodded. 'That's if Bignose is still boss man in this neck of the woods.'

She reined down sharply, her horse moving restlessly under her. 'Bignose!'

'Yeah – that is his bailiwick. Or was – if he survived that wagon blast he's likely still the *jefe* around these parts. Or some other bandit with ambitions might have killed him and taken over the leadership.'

'But there is a chance – a chance we might yet meet up with this Bignose?'

'I won't be going out of my way to cross his path.'

'No – of course not. But if we are near his camp...'

'Forget it. For a start I have no idea where his hideout is and I don't want to know. I'm all for making as fast a run as possible to the Border – and to hell with Bignose.'

She stared hard at him and then nodded gently. '*Sí*, you wish to remain uninvolved, eh? While we pass by the man who killed my father!'

Rio blinked. 'Thought you had me down for that job. Don't tell me you finally believe me.'

That jaw thrust out once again and she looked positively haughty. 'Perhaps I know you a little better now, Rio.'

'Whatever that means,' he muttered and then touched his spurs to the palomino's flanks. 'Let's go, Rosita. This is no place to be caught by a bunch of bandits.'

She agreed with that and spurred after him.

They rode for two days, on edge, stopping constantly to check the country for pursuers. Twice Rio saw dust clouds behind but they were well over to the east and quite a way back. They might not have had anything to do with them. But it was a sign that even in this wilderness they were not alone.

'Where do you make contact with your friends?' Rio asked as they rode through timber fringing a placid lake that reflected sky and trees one afternoon.

'I was given the name of the town. I have San Antonio in mind but that can't be right. That is in Texas, no?'

'There's a San Antonio de Bravos on the

Mexican side of the Border ... known as "Bravo" to most folk.'

'*Si! Si!* That is the place! You know this?'

He nodded, studying her. 'Yeah – it was where I had to make contact after the wet back run. Feller sent down by someone named Barnaby–'

She sucked in a breath sharply. 'You – know of this Barnaby?'

He nodded, deciding not to tell her that they were enemies. 'I was surprised to find he was involved with Mexican rebels.'

'Ah! He is no one to be trusted. He wants many acres of land south of the Rio Grande in payment for his help. He thinks he is using us for his own ends but we will use *him* until we do not need him anymore.'

'Uh-huh – well, let's get going. We camp tonight around the far side of the *lago* and I think we can make Bravo by sundown tomorrow.'

'*Bueno!* And then what, Rio?'

His eyes narrowed. 'I've told you enough times,' he said gruffly and rode on.

She followed, looking thoughtful. 'You are sure you cannot cross into Texas?'

'No! And that's final. Hell, even if Holt was dead, it still wouldn't matter. The sonuver used his influence to have me charged with murder and that warrant would still be out, whether he's around or not.'

'If you could prove you killed only in self-defence...'

He snorted. 'With my reputation? Forget it, Rosita – I see you safely to Bravo and then I'm off to Vera Cruz, hell or high water.'

She fell silent then as they rode slowly around the lake, even more beautiful with sunset colours.

He didn't want a fire in the camp but she insisted after looking at his wound.

'It is filthy! It needs a good clean and the hot water will help bring down the swelling. There is some pus, Rio – it must be painful.'

'Get on with it,' he growled, and watched as she collected twigs and kindling and got a small fire going. After she had cleaned the wound – and he had to admit it did feel way better – she made coffee.

It was while they were drinking their second cup each that the bandits came into the camp.

They moved like ghosts and when Rio spotted the first man, dropped his cup and stood, hand slapping his gun butt, he felt a rifle muzzle ram against his spine. He stopped dead and the girl cried out, jumping to her feet.

Suddenly there were five men surrounding them, all armed, and then a sixth man came out of the shadows, breathing with wheezing sounds. There was no doubt as to his identity.

Firelight reflected dully from the greasy sweat on his large nose. He was breathing with his mouth partly open and Rio could see the tops of filthy bandages showing at the neck of his open, threadbare shirt.

'Ah, the gringo with the dynamite!' he said to Rio, thrusting him hard on the shoulder. 'So you survived, too. You one clever son of a bitch, eh? You nearly finish me.'

'Let me try again,' Rio said and Bignose

grinned with gapped, tobacco-stained teeth.

'I think I will not, gringo – you are one tough *hombre* as well as clever. I hear about you. You kill Luis Banda, and a man I know – *knew* – Señor Bodine. I know you pretty damn good to do these things.'

'You are well informed, *jefe*,' Rio said carefully, knowing how unstable this man was.

'Ah, I know.' He tapped his big nose and waited, perhaps expecting a wisecrack and ready to punish it, but Rio said nothing. 'Many things – I have many eyes and ears. They tell me of the bank robbery in Los Sequito – the masked man who spoke Spanish with an *americano* accent. Who take hostage a beautiful *señorita* suppose to be the *alcalde's amante...*'

The girl flushed angrily. 'I am no man's mistress, damn you! I am Rosita de Ayora.'

Bignose smiled again, and Rio realized that the smile that showed those huge, mossy-looking teeth, made the man uglier than ever.

'This I also know *señorita*. I believe I have

the pleasure not so long ago of killing your father.' He made a mock bow in her direction, too amused and intent on playing the fool to notice the genuine hatred and anger boiling in her. 'Now I will kill you – but not right away. I will make sure it is even *more* pleasure to kill you!'

'Pig!' she spat at him. 'You will die for murdering my father.'

'I will die sometime, as we all must, but not for anything I did to your father – or to you. I intend to live a long time yet.' Then he spun swiftly and a big fist caught Rio off-guard as the hard knuckles crashed across the side of his head. He staggered and the man with the rifle who had been covering him jumped back, startled. Bignose laughed and added, 'And I will live well! Because you have *mucho dinero* for me, eh, gringo? You bring it specially for me, eh?'

Rio sighed, feeling the split inside his mouth with the tip of his tongue. 'I was hoping to surprise you with it, *jefe*.'

The girl glared at him. He shrugged.

'Hell, Rosita, I told you this was his country – you gotta be prepared to pay your way to such men as the *jefe* here. You must show him respect – or be ready to pay the consequences, right, *jefe?*'

Bignose looked wary but he nodded, not taking his eyes from Rio's face. 'You were going to give me the *dinero?* All of it?'

'Well, I thought you might let us keep enough to get to Bravo and bribe our way across the Border...'

The girl tensed, knowing at his words that this was some kind of a trick. She had to be ready to help – whatever Rio was planning. And she couldn't even begin to think what it might be. Not with six armed men surrounding them.

'Now why should I care whether you get across the Border or not, gringo? Anyway, it is said you dare not cross the Rio Grande into the *Estado Unidos.* I think maybe I decide how much to leave you after I see the money, gringo–'

Rio shook his head. 'No good, chief. We

make the deal first, then I get the money.'

'Get the money? You have it with you! Look at your saddle-bags!'

'They bulge with food and clothes, *jefe*. We buried the money along the trail.'

'You lie!' Bignose roared, gasping, eyes wide, a little spittle showing at the corner of his mouth. He lunged at Rio, swinging his big fists and the two men closest with rifles hurriedly stepped back.

It left Rio standing clear, for the moment no guns actually trained on him...

Then the girl screamed as, too fast for her to see, a gun blazed in his hand and two men staggered and dropped their rifles and fell groaning. Bignose, quicker than a rattler, threw another man at Rio who dived headlong, killed the luckless peon and swung his gun towards the bandit chief.

Bignose started running, but he grabbed the girl by the arm first and the remaining two Mexicans fired at Rio as he rolled across the ground, through the camp fire, scattering blazing brands. With lead kicking dust and stones around him, he blasted them both. Bignose drew his gun and yanked the girl towards him for a shield.

She went with him willingly and as Bignose threw down on Rio – whose gun was empty now – she drove her knife to the hilt between his ribs. He froze, his gun exploding and jumping from his hand. Wide-eyed, he turned his head towards her and she looked calmly up into his face, withdrew the knife – and plunged it home again into the middle of his chest.

His weight tore the weapon from her grip and Bignose sprawled, thrashing his last, as the echoes of the gunfire died away.

Rio sat up and then stood, shucking shells from his gunbelt and replacing the used cartridges in his Colt. The six bandits' bodies sprawled in various uncomfortable-looking positions around the camp which was quite dark now, lit only by the remnants of the campfire.

He holstered his gun and went to Bignose's body to retrieve the girl's knife, saying, 'Well, you've avenged your father now, Rosita.'

'Sí – I feel better. But I will feel even more better when you give me that *dinero* in your saddle-bags, Rio!'

He spun, leaving the knife still in Bignose. She held Bignose's gun that she had picked up, the hammer cocked, the weapon held in both hands.

'Now, Rosita, how come you're so greedy all of a sudden?'

She shook her head quickly. 'It is not for me! It is for my *compadres!*'

'The *renegados?*'

'Call them *revolucionarios!*'

'Still the same killers.' He saw her eyes narrow. She firmed her grip on the Colt. 'The money's mine, Rosita.'

'I helped you get it! I let you take me hostage!'

He sighed again. 'Had a notion it might come down to this, but I figured once we got to Bravo – look, Rosita, I was going to split it with you. You've been through plenty and you're damn near a fanatic. I can get by with two thirds.'

'Oh? I am to get only one third?'

'I was the one had to face Bodine's gun.' Suddenly he made a savage gesture with his left hand and she instinctively swung her gun that way. Then she jumped and yelped as his own Colt blazed and a bullet tore the gun from her grasp. She snatched at her numbed wrist, bent almost double.

'That bullet could just as easily have gone through your heart, Rosita. Let's not stand here like a couple of kids in the school yard squabbling over the spoils of some escapade. I have the money. I've lost a lot more one way and another. You know the way to Bravo now and whoever you're supposed to contact, so, I think the time has come for us to say farewell.'

She looked at him and her face softened. 'Rio – I *need* some of that money! There is so much to do – and for a man like you, so good with a pistol–' She paused and spread her hands. 'The rewards will be great when we overthrow *El Presidente*. Won't you come with me and join us, Rio?'

He holstered his gun and turned to the palomino, picking up his saddle and blanket and throwing them across the patient animal's back.

'You go?' she said, obviously disappointed. 'You will not reconsider?'

He swung up into the saddle after tying his warbag behind the cantle, looking at her standing there amongst the dead men. He reached into a saddlebag, brought out a canvas sack with the Los Sequito bank's name stencilled on the side and tossed it at her feet.

'*Adios,* Rosita,' he said as he turned the horse.

'No – *hasta luego,* Rio!' She clasped the bag of cash to her. 'Till next time.'

He paused, shook his head slightly. 'No, just *adios.*'

Farewell...

Then he started down the slope away from the camp and the girl, heading south.

She called his name, taking a step after him. He did not give any sign that he had heard.

Just before he disappeared into the darkness of the heavy timber down there, she knew he was right.

They would never meet again.

'Much luck, Rio!' she called. 'Much luck – *amigo!*'